RAIN NEVER FELL

RAIN NEVER FELL

By Alaine Laws

LONGSHORE
REBEL

PRESS

Book cover by Alaine Laws.

ISBN 979-8-9985500-5-8 (paperback)

First edition January 2026.

This one is for Erin, who wants a better world, not one where no spring flows nor rain ever fell.

RAIN NEVER FELL

Cabo Verde

THE WEATHER broadcaster wasn't the only one watching the storm.

The day it showed up as a tropical wave, anyone with a compcorder or even just a wristcomp could see it off the coast of Africa and speculate about whether envireng would choose it to relieve the drought—they couldn't steer it; nobody could do that. But if the wind currents were favorable for sending it over a needy part of the country, and if it contained water to be seeded out…that, they could manage. Wringing clouds out like soaked linen coming from a washtub, that, they could manage. It had been done, for more than a century and a half.

And everyone knew envireng would do it ethically, responsibly. Those words were in the opening sentence of its charter, going back more than eighty years.

It is stipulated that the herein named Department of Environmental Engineering shall be governed by all ordinances, rules, and laws formulated by the overseeing Committee for Responsible and Ethical Social Stewardship.

"CRESS." The revolutionary students called it "CRASS." An old word, but it meant a lot, in its time.

Cabo Verde

INSURGENT 35 had a lot of the stuff, a lot, more than he'd ever need, really; but it had been too good a deal to pass up, offered as it was by the nervous envireng worker who knew somebody'd tapped into the stockpile record and had started asking secret questions. 35 had the documents—they were pretty much public knowledge, the agency forced into openness after the last subsistence drought and catastrophe.

35 and his comrades sneered always at that phrase, "subsistence drought." It was so in character for envireng to call it a "drought," a lack of rain, which was something *they* could sometimes adjust to society's benefit. In reality it had been a lack of everything—clothing, food, housing, medicine, fuel, anything one needed to subsist on. Alleviating *that* was beyond their power. But saying it was a "drought" kindled hope, reminded people that envireng could, yes, bring extra rain at times, and therefore might be able to bring calm and order as well. Have faith in them.

"Have faith in them," 35 and his companions jeered whenever a new fuel or food restriction was issued, using that word on purpose. He'd done his undergrad work on psyphi itself, on how the agency manipulated words and memory, on how it employed its own version of what they used to call "subliminal advertising."

35 also did his own experiments on the chemical, tinkered with the concentration amounts, ran current through it—high current, producing lots of ozone, subjected his carefully-documented mixtures to the kind of humidity you'd find in coastal West Africa, where most of those storms originated, anyway.

And he'd added some things.

One day, 19, not knowing 35 was at work, opened the door. "Loscadh is dó ort!"—more vulgar curses not being considered ethical anymore, they'd found useful, exotic ones in a long-extinct language. The sudden change in room climate, the drop in humidity as cooler and drier air rushed in, had nearly ruined that experiment. He swore good-naturedly back—"Droch chrích ort!"— and scrupulously recorded the altered parameters, because they did produce strange results after he resumed, though he was never able to duplicate that particular trial.

He'd nearly killed himself half a dozen times. If he'd succeeded in doing it, that would've been sacrifice for the greater good, he thought. Sometimes the glass containers he used had shimmered and burst, and he'd dashed from the room he called his lab, watched through the four-ply glastique window as a billowy cloud arose from the shattered vessels, turned slightly orange and rained down upon absorbent papers. All the liquid soaked up, but slowly, spreading outward little by little, tentacles creeping along as if searching for something.

After a few times, when he figured out the right amount of electricity to add, he'd put a couple of white mice near the glastique containers, tiny, sweet little things, really, and he regretted it, but science was science. When the vessel shattered and the glowing rain fell, the mice would shiver a little, sit back, look upward, seemingly at peace, as blood emptied out of their ears, eyes, mouths, noses, anuses. They never struggled. 35 noted that it seemed not a bad way to die.

Or sometimes they were indifferent and just turned orange later. But those expired in a couple of weeks.

Or sometimes they screamed tiny little cries and scratched on their eyes and ears before falling over.

The seller, wanting him to think it was top-secret information, gave him envireng experiment records, too, a package deal, he'd said. 35 scoffed to let the man know he or anybody could get those records off the net. Envireng had been **ethically**, **responsibly** transparent. Still, the documents gave him a starting point for his own work. And he'd learned from them to take special precautions for his own safety. So: not only the haz-mat lab suit he purchased unreported, but the four-ply glastique panel in the door, and the powerful vacuum system to clean up, afterwards.

If he succeeded, envireng would eventually find him. They always did—the price exacted for universal transparency was that no one had secrets very long—and there'd be a quick trial, because he wouldn't contest anything. But, anyway, they wouldn't off him; they didn't do that anymore. Besides, he kept one ace card in the game for himself: He'd tell them he'd been exposed, too, and then they'd take his meticulous records for further study and keep him somewhere safe, to be watched, a controlled experiment himself.

Latitude N 13.9
Longitude W 51
Wind Speed 94 knots

WILLIAM CONNOR, the news broadcaster, called storms "beasts."

During those two and a half weeks, news scrolling across one side on the wall screen, graphics in the middle, David would add his commentary in a deep voice, posh accent straight from the twentieth century. He did it mostly when Victoria happened to be in the same room with him and Catherine, and she'd sigh in disgust and roll her eyes, toss her head so the white feathers swirled around her brows.

"This beast, born in the Azores, has been pretty tame so far and is unlikely to be a serious menace because of the steering currents and wind shear in this area." Connor gestured at sections of the radar maps behind him.

"So what shall we do?" David pontificated, pointing here and there in a robotic manner. "Inoculate it with our chemicals and make it useful and coincidentally dangerous? 'Tame' is so boring."

"Stop, David," Catherine would say with an uncomfortable laugh. It bothered her when he was flippant. No, not that, exactly: sardonic, irreverent? Though "irreverent" wasn't a word used much anymore.

"Ugh." Victoria would make an "O" of her middle finger and thumb, snap them apart almost in a thump near his face. Sometimes he would frown at the insult, sometimes just slap her hand away and chuckle. Even knowing it was obscene, meant to embody a man being violently spurned from having sex.

"We shall give it a name," he droned along.

Hurricanes hadn't been named in a long time. They were numbers now.

He leaned forward, rubbing his hands together like a mad scientist. Victoria made claws and clutched at the air around her face before leaving the room with a shriek.

"You think they'll pick this one?" Catherine asked.

His eyes turned from the split screen to her then, and his voice was light. "Probably. If they're right, it'll weaken some in a few days, and they'll squeeze out all that water. This region can use it, you know." He turned back to the screens, eyes squinted a little, and one side of his mouth turned upward into the mockery of a smile. "It shall be productive; we shall make it so," he intoned over the voice of Connor.

She heard Victoria slamming out of the house.

Latitude N 34.5
Longitude W 78
Wind Speed 79 knots

i

SEVERAL PUBLIC transports wheezed with drawn-out, soft sighs to a stop in the lot in front of Catherine's sanction van. She juggled Virginia from her left hip to her right, waiting for clearance to enter the domed observation area. Enormous plastic banners hung over the entrances, welcoming them.

Preparing it all had consumed every day and night of the storm's journey from Cape Verde westward, had taken sums of money people strenuously questioned and university students protested. How could the economy be so grim if there were resources for all this?

Yet resources had been found, money spent, workmen compensated with account bonuses. And David wanted her to be there when the outer bands first crossed the coastline. Envireng had arranged for the under-coords to have their moment, "in the sun," the cheerful manager had added, using an antiquated term for "of celebrity." He picked the phrase on purpose, trying to be humorously relevant, given the circumstances today, a deliberate choice driven by a goal of rehabilitating the agency's reputation.

Last week the same envireng manager scheduled a video broadcast and brought David in to explain that, because of the chemical properties of the dome, people chosen to observe would see a mother-of-pearl effect through the glastique. Catherine, watching the broadcast at home with Victoria standing behind her, scoffing throughout the whole thing, had thought David did well: no obvious nervousness, his words reassuringly plain. Yes, Victoria, it was scripted, no doubt there. But he'd made it sound unscripted.

A final syllable of derision, and Victoria left the room, her white hair waving.

He'd done what envireng wanted: He'd exemplified the calm tech that he was, that the agency wanted people to remember…but with that human touch.

There'd been so much referencing of colors—of the iridescent observation dome, the potential for purple-shaded clouds, the hues of the sunsets on two or three days following the storm—as if colors would make up for the rain that fell steadily in wind-blown sheets like sheer grey curtains today.

So: a day of heavy, much-needed rain to quench the drought, a little wind, yes, but then lovely sunsets.

Victoria called chirpy educational broadcasts "brainwashing," an old-fashioned term she was misusing, David told her.

"A happy bonus. Three brilliant sunsets, or maybe even four, maybe four lovely sunsets," David had explained.

The envireng manager had loved that and repeated it: "Happy bonus!" A comment resonant of reward-for-responsibility was always appreciated. David had hoped it would translate into an actual account bonus for him, though so far it hadn't; but they had allowed him, no, *encouraged* him to bring his family to observe the procedure today, and so he'd gently nagged Catherine to be there, with Virginia. It would look good for him, and, sometime or other, might actually result in an account boost.

She hadn't wanted to come. She was well versed in the whole envireng-benefit doctrine—"brainwashed," Victoria would say; but there'd always been in the back of her mind a disquietude about the whole event. It was just pulled together too fast, she fretted. It was like—she'd hesitated, not wanting to use the dated term, but nothing else came to her mind—it was like tempting fate.

David scoffed, not disrespectfully as Victoria would, but with a smile and one word: "Superstitious?"

She shrugged and agreed with him: "Maybe." She didn't mention the queasiness had been inherited from her grandfather: David would become grave and disapproving....

Virginia waved her bottle of juice, squirmed, kicked her feet against Catherine's deep pocket. With her free hand Catherine fumbled and drew out the ring heavy with bits of metal: antique keys, one of the baby's favorite toys.

"You have to carry so many things, with a baby," a woman nearby said. "Something to entertain, their food..." The thin smile stayed on her lips as her brows lowered a little. "She your only?"

"She has a sister. An older sister." Catherine glanced around for a reason to move away.

"I don't remember you on the transport."

So there it was, expected, and she knew she flinched. "No."

The woman glanced again at Virginia. "Surely didn't bike in with her." She waited, not turning away, aggressive in polite, silent insistence.

Catherine gestured at the lot: Let her make her own assumptions.

The woman turned to gaze at the basic, no-frills sanction van parked behind the public transports. Catherine waited for some expression of resentment; there usually was one at that point.

Virginia had watched the entire exchange with quiet interest and suddenly reached down into the deep pocket to pull out the keyring and, incidentally, a few tiny copper disks as well, which dropped onto the floor and spun around for a few seconds before lying flat.

The woman whispered to someone standing at her side.

So now the group around her here at Site Three would think she was not only eccentric but possibly a criminal, involved with unreported purchasing. The coins lay untouched head's-up on the floor. She shifted Virginia and bent to pick them up.

She wouldn't have cared at all if she hadn't known that the people weren't random—they'd all been selected, at first glance just a mixture of mostly young families—you, yes, and you with the healthy baby—and distinguished, robust older citizens—no one at the age should apply for a pass, please—but they were there, Catherine knew, as scenic backdrop for the broadcast. They were chosen, so that the newscaster wandering around the periphery at the moment could, without speaking, merely by swinging an arm towards the loud baby or the healthy elders, remind viewers of the success and ethics of envireng policy.

Others were chosen, too; so he could turn to the thin, suited man near Catherine who looked like an accountant and conduct an apparently spontaneous interview on his opinion of the advantages of the procedure. Or ask questions of the dark-haired young woman in the uniform that suspiciously resembled the ones Victoria's classmates wore, and elicit the idealistic ruminations of a schoolteacher.

—Except that the thin, suited man, Catherine knew, was the project coordinator in charge today, the "over-coord." And the "schoolteacher" in the uniform had designed the dome of glastique that would, from their perspective underneath, look like mother-of-pearl and protect them from the weather.

Envireng had even provided the sanction public transports, an expensive concession.

David had told her all this—a flouting of directives, but he always told her everything, knowing she'd keep it to herself. Envireng was counting on today's production to redeem themselves, to expunge from the collective national memory images of the insurgents they'd accidentally killed decades earlier. This would be, David said, like one of the old space launches of the previous century, when resources still allowed those events. There were few bigscale public entertainments now, and so envireng had given passes to observe the procedure, as if it were an old-fashioned fireworks exhibition to honor a long forgotten festival; or—he gazed mischievously at Victoria—one of those nuclear detonations, where people had lined up to watch the mushroom cloud form. Hadn't she mentioned that in her recent school paper, the one her instructor marked up? But there was no danger in today's procedure. Harvesting rain didn't work well every time, but mostly it helped in drought-stricken areas.

People even used to perform rain dances, even had public prayers, he'd added, a final joke to tease her. She'd made the obscene gesture at him again.

He said the interviews planned for today were specially arranged for special reasons, a carefully-designed psyphi effort to educate against the backdrop of the drought-breaking rain. So the thin man and uniformed woman had been shuttled to Site Three on the rear bench of Catherine's sanction van, mysteriously aloof, with two under-coords. Catherine resented sharing her own vehicle with people she did not know, was annoyed at not being able even to ask their names, but David had shrugged. He reminded her it was a part of their deal. Their responsibility for consuming.

They were acquainted with one of the under-coords, had even considered traveling together on holiday, but Gregory didn't care for the beach and at last removed himself from their plans. When he folded his lanky body into the van, he'd patted her back. Then the suited man and the uniformed woman got in, sitting together but never acknowledging anyone else's or even each other's presence, their eyes hooded, darting sideways, glancing suspiciously but secretly at one another as they faced ahead. The van was ominously quiet; the uniformed woman had tapped her fingers constantly on the edge of the window next to her, and the suited man absent-mindedly caressed a large, expensive-looking ring on his left hand.

Catherine wished she hadn't been required to bring them. But they had responsibilities today, too.

She glanced at one of the large display screens suspended from the ceiling of the observation grandstand. Each screen aired scenes from a different sector: The control shelter, a defiantly flimsy three-sided booth constructed entirely of transparent glastique, where she could observe David's consultations with the other under-coords and his brief, occasional glances toward the screen for her benefit (he'd promised to do that). The domed observation grandstand she and Virginia occupied with the broadcast crew and the other invited people. Victoria's school, where students garbed in rain gear had been herded under another of the hut-like shelters, to watch and take notes—a science outing, in a seeded hurricane, fun, Victoria had mocked. The final screen displayed a view of the dome overhead, its iridescence shining in the dripping rain and lightning flashes. That screen seemed redundant, as they stood under the dome itself. Maybe it was for the benefit of people watching from their homes.

She remembered this morning before David left; they'd been drinking tea and watching this same constant view on their wall screen. It's like a pearl, she said.

He'd laughed: No, it's not—it's like a great big blister.

Don't say that out loud. Blisters burst.

From here it did look like a blister, she thought now, a huge blister on the skin of the earth, and they were underneath the blister, and it looked fragile. And the control booth where David and his colleagues were sheltered—it looked like one of the huts from the subsistence drought that she'd seen images of, thrown up all over the place by the angry homeless. Too small.

David kissed her and even stole a brief hug from Victoria as he left. The control booth was only a rain shelter, he said, that, and nothing else. It was constructed to shoulder against the wind. The rain wouldn't be cold. They'd all be wearing heavy raingear. Glastique was by now a reliable, proven material. They'd be adequately shielded from the dying hurricane. He gave her all the points he'd made in his broadcast appearance. Things were controlled, planned carefully, as Victoria had been, as Virginia had been. Everything was considered.

Victoria shuddered elaborately in her snide, adolescent way. "Then why'd you put Mom and Gin at Site Three? Why not right there with you?"

David was patient with his rebellious daughter, more patient than Catherine herself, she thought, and he explained: "It wouldn't look good for her to be there with me, just because I could get her there."

Victoria said to his back, but quietly, "*Mallacht Dé ort.*"

David laughed. " '*Dé*'? Superstitious, a little?"

Catherine turned to reprimand her, but Victoria held up a palm. "Save the lecture."

"Do you have your pager?"

With an exaggerated flourish, Victoria had pressed a button on the small device. Lights flickered across the relay dish mounted on the wall, and she turned again to brandish the positioner now in Catherine's face and left for school. Her wispy bleached hair floating out behind her like emu feathers.

One final word: "*Diabhalta.*"

"If anything goes wrong," David mused as she flung herself out the door, "like, maybe the storm gets stronger or something, the control shelter ought to be thick enough." Catherine glanced at him, noting the doubt, and he shrugged: "I almost reminded her about that, but she probably already knows, and, anyway, nothing's going wrong. That's why they put me there, to make sure. Sorry we have to bring those others along, but we all have to be there. And we may get bonuses from it if everything goes right." He frowned. " '*When*' everything goes right."

ii

THERE WAS some bustling around. Broadcast crew tactfully moved people here, over there, away from the tall man in the dark suit who stood disdainfully at the edge of the grandstand, pulling up his sleeve to check his wristcomp with impatient frequency. Catherine realized that people holding the noisy babies and toddlers were being grouped into a corner well away from the man, but still close enough to see the screens.

Virginia waved her juice and spilled a little on Catherine's new pants, allowed as a special luxury bonus for having been thrifty during the previous quarter. She grimaced; but perhaps they wouldn't be too hard to clean.

Her eyes turned back and forth from the screen on which David still glanced upward once in a while, a tiny curve on his lips for her amusement, and the one showing small groups of canvas-covered students carrying standard-issue compcorders. They all looked alike except for height, their faces obscured by the overhanging weatherproof hoods.

Victoria assured them both she would not be looking up. But, then, none of the students were.

Four spotlights suddenly assaulted the tall man, who straightened his shoulders and dropped the disdainful expression, focusing on a prompter set with the first lines of his planned commentary. Catherine observed the pre-broadcast countdown and last-minute adjustments to take advantage of the theatricality of the howling wind and dark clouds, and turned back to look for Victoria's lowered head on the screens.

All four were suddenly appropriated by the image of the tall man. "William Connor at Site Three, under the dome. Rain is intensifying here, and we're all glad to be dry." He gestured toward the top of the blister, which did indeed appear made of thin oyster shell as rain swirled upon it, running down in multi-patterned rivers precipitated by ominously gray-purple clouds.

"I have with me Micaela Sánchez, who designs biodomes and will explain later some interesting things about where they're used. And Sebastian Franklin dropped by to tell us a little about weather systems.

"Earlier today the aircraft with its enormous cargo of silver iodide passed through and over multiple bands of the storm. What we're witnessing now is relief from the multi-year drought in this area, or so it is to be hoped. Calculations are ongoing—" another gesture, and cameras turned to Site One and the three-sided control shelter where David stared at compcorder screens— "to record this event for future study."

The spectators listened to the monologue as he continued saying what scrolled off the prompter, and Catherine watched the screens, noting that David's glances upward were less frequent.

"In the last subsistence drought, when the deadly chemical branded 'Eutopix' led to accidentally tragic consequences, environmental engineering's reputation took a hit. It's hoped today's rainfall intervention will help restore viewers' confidence."

He deviated from the script—Catherine, glancing at the prompter right then, saw he ad-libbed the next words: "So far, everything seems to be going as was hoped. This beast's brought us some really deplorable weather! Wish they *could* control it."

The winds seemed stronger, cloud bands more tightly wound now, lightning a frequent assault.

"As what's called the 'eye' approaches," Connor went on, "home viewers will notice that here at Site Three we're having sixty mile-an-hour winds and driving rain which we're told will supply remedy for the several-years' deficit.

"You may have wondered about the different locations from which things are being managed and observed. Site One is for mission-critical people, the under-coords monitoring and recording all aspects of this event. Site Two, something less than half a kilometer away from Site One, is where university and upper-quad students are actively observing as a portion of their coursework. Site Three, where this broadcast originates, is most removed from what once would have been called 'ground zero,' a place designated for the general public. We have the driest view, as you see, but perhaps the least exciting." He allowed a wry smile. The uniformed young woman who'd come with Catherine turned cynical eyes on him.

But as if envireng had arranged it, winds unexpectedly hammered the dome, the heavy clouds swirled around in a violent circular direction, lightning was drawn into the various collectors nearby. In spite of herself, Catherine shut her eyes and winced.

Lightning's not our concern anymore, David had told her. We learned a long time ago about electricity and lightning and how to channel it to the power grid. Nothing's going to get hit by lightning—and, seeing her flinch as a tremendous bolt crashed down somewhere just as they wheeled into the parking lot today, he pointed at the two white-uniformed security guards, each supplied with the dull pewter cylinder of a charge gun. *We understand electricity now. Stop worrying about lightning.*

The storm howled. Connor's face was demonic with energy and pleasure.

Broadcast engineers switched again to a view of the control booth, where, Catherine noted, the impish glances upward had ceased.

Lights overhead in the grandstand area flickered twice. The

generator-driven halogen lights garishly illuminating Connor did not waver.

The students clicked away on their compcorders harnessed to their waistlines with nylon and aluminum frames. On the afternoon of the day long ago when she'd had her own compcorder assigned to her, Victoria had come home mocking the solemn lecture given the students concerning their equipment: *And this story about soldiers back in war times getting their weapons and how their weapons were like a part of them, and these things were a part of us now, and we were always to have them with us, take care of them*.

She'd waved the machine in the air over her head like a cheap cap.

Catherine turned her attention to Connor, now that David was too busy to look up. Broadcast engineers were making delicate adjustments to the tulip microphone, opening its petal-like sections to gather more of Connor's voice, pointing the inner micro-catcher of a pistil at him. He gestured expansively. His eyes glittered with enthusiasm.

The screen shifted to the shelter under which serious techs twisted knobs and calibrated measurements.

"Synchronized with the inner, most intense storm bands," Connor went on, "to maximize the upward draft and distribute it into the upper atmosphere, under-engineers are adding a final dose of enhanced silver iodide to the storm even now, in an effort to wring out more moisture."

Virginia clutched Catherine's neck at a sudden increase in the shrill scream of the wind. Catherine held her tightly against the press of the crowd, her eyes on the four screens that showed split views of Connor and the control shelter.

On a thin display behind David's head, bright red numbers counted downward from ten.

The students with the compcorders tapped, looked up.

Lightning flashed, a tremendous bolt nearby making the spectators blink and cower and the lights go dim. In the booth the under-coords compensated for it, and the one that followed, pressing buttons, recording data.

Another lightning bolt. Another momentary power blink. More adjustments, as a stream of glastique cylinders shot upward from around the control shelter, at first a few, then more and more, perhaps close to fifty, all breaking through the cloud layers like small rockets, disappearing from sight.

"And there they go!"

The milling crowd gasped quietly, applauded a little.

The students gathered hoods nearer their faces and looked at screens in their shelter.

"Look—I think it's a twister!" someone shrieked.

Arrangements had also been worked out for this possibility—it was always possible, with hurricane weather systems like this one, the broadcast envireng had conceded, tornadoes not predictable despite environmental quality's best efforts. Extra rain could be provided, but tornadoes were springs popping out of an antique clock. The underbelly of the nearer clouds was pregnant, a squirming, whirling appendage trying to burst free. As one, the crowd of spectators moaned and herded themselves obediently toward a door painted with a corkscrew symbol, leading down into a synthetic-walled cave that had been hastily buried as an afterthought, when the storm had begun its turn toward the region.

"I thought they'd already flown the plane." A woman in front of Catherine pointed to a screen.

Catherine turned to see, yes, it was an airplane, silver, with a green-and-purple hexagonal symbol on its nose, breaking through clouds, swinging lower over the control site. Very low. Too low. Nose down.

The uniformed dome designer shoved spectators out of her way as she also approached and glared wide-eyed and frozen.

"It's blowing orange smoke—" this from a child behind Catherine. "Look, it's got orange smoke." She was delighted. More colors.

The crowd milled uncertainly between the shelter door and the grandstand where the broadcast continued, unnarrated; Connor, his apocalyptic remarks now interrupted, was watching the screens, a detached, mildly interested expression on his face. Half a kilometer away the dark cloud travailed to birth the writhing thing.

"I warned you," the dome designer said scornfully to the project coordinator who stumbled up behind her. "I told you somebody'd—"

The noise of the crash covered other words as the plane blew up in a fireball a stadium-field away from Site One.

iii

WHAT THE child called "smoke" coalesced into a blanket of orange smog that wafted upwards fast, amazingly fast, into the belly of the storm, as if vacuumed upwards, as if multiplying itself exponentially.

Insurgent 35 watched the broadcast in his lab and was gratified to see his theories about neptunium confirmed. He'd never been fool enough himself to run that particular trial. But in real time, today, he was watching his idea, *his*, realized on a large scale.

He felt vindicated. Some of the others had never believed he'd properly documented his procedures, had said that was why he couldn't always explain his results.

The green-and-purple hexagon was theirs, a sort of Jesus fish they could use as the final part of their elaborate safe-code verification—though that had to change now, 35 reflected, since it had been painted on the stolen aircraft for all the world to see.

The group was only tenuously connected, the better to maintain deniability, and they liked using numbers instead of names. 35 had known vague parameters of the plan, knew a plane would be loaded with the stuff, would dump it when the storm was strong over Site One. The pilot, an acquaintance of his, may have tried to circle around and leave, but 35 knew he wasn't much of a pilot. And, anyway, if he'd been exposed, himself, to the chemical he was dumping on that *diabhalta* group, he may have already been dead long before the plane hit the ground.

35 thought again, Not a bad way to die. He'd done the work, fine-tuned it to be that way. A small handful of the others had always questioned the need for another mass kill-off, and one had even made the mistake of using that word, "ethical," bringing great ridicule on himself. A shame, that that once-legitimate query had been appropriated by envireng, so that now nobody else could use it without sounding like a mouthpiece for the agency.

iv

ONE OF the engineers shifted the broadcast into a slow, automatic mode so that the four huge screens were alternately filled with images first of Connor, an inappropriately amused slight smile on his face; then Site Twos, students clicking away at their compcorders, still busily taking notes as instructed; and Site Ones, where confused faces frowned and murmurs echoed through the tulip micro-catchers, and David's coworkers with him twisted knobs and slid levers up and down and gesticulated wildly. And finally, the view upward at their dome where a mother-of-pearl and orange brew swirled and crept down the outside wall, and, at the top, large pieces had been blown away. Catherine thought, But we're not that close to the crash site, why is it broken? It was an irrational, almost angry thought, as if she'd been inconvenienced somehow. Rain and billowy, glowing wisps began to trail through the hole, then more, as a second explosion enlarged the hole, and large diaphanous shreds drifted downward.

Virginia pointed gleefully and said, "Pitty! Pitty!" Fissures raced down the sides of the blister.

The autopan returned to Connor, whose expression was now mild irritation. The crowd grew impatient with the slow progression of the images through all four scenes and surged to the walls of the burst dome in a futile effort to peer through the wind-blown drenching rain outside to see the flaming aircraft. Catherine felt the jostling but could not remove her eyes from the screens.

Teenagers at Site Two, holding out their arms to an orange rain as if they thought this another aspect of the experiment to be analyzed later in class.

Panicked exodus at Site One; but also the under-coordinators huddled against one of the walls inside their shelter, rubbing their hands.

"David!"

She had not intended to say it aloud, but the uniformed woman heard and edged away. "Dada," Virginia echoed. Catherine mutely urged him to look up, as if he could hear her, and then yanked Virginia's head firmly down on her shoulder when he did, a horrific, slack look of druggy peace stretching his mouth into a crooked smile as blood oozed from his facial orifices.

The airplane burned on, in spite of the rain, and the handful of rescue workers who'd initially sprinted over now lay on the ground nearby. Low clouds that twisted and wrung about tried to birth tornadoes; clouds sucked in the orange mist and changed, spread and grew.

The autopan shifted back to Connor.

"It's probably inside the storm system now. Stay out of the rain. You all need to go to your designated shelters for a few days." The uniformed woman spoke calmly, dispassionately to people near her.

The crowd mumbled then: "Didn't you design this thing?" "That's what they said earlier."

She stood her ground in front of the screens, now airing the deserted Site One, an electronic panel with flashing readouts and red smears on the glastique walls of the shelter. Someone had turned off the camera at Site Two; ten seconds of grey blankness took the place of the students. As the scene again shifted to the remnants of the blister-dome, the woman cursed and pulled the master cable, and all the screens went black.

"Whatever that is will dissolve in the rain and fall back down," she continued, calm but loud. Like a teacher. "Everybody should leave. Now. If you can. Stay out of the rain," she repeated.

Catherine stood near the black screens as the crowd hesitantly at first and then with energized terror streamed around her to the exits, or to the tornado shelter door. A loud hum followed by an urgent shriek accompanied one of the public transports as its driver overrode the sensors to whirl from the lot, the bus only half-full. Seeing this, the other spectators streamed to the lot and the re-maining public transports. The dome designer grabbed the suited man's arm. "Where're you going?"

"Plane's still on fire. The two of you could immolate yourselves," Connor said dryly.

Catherine watched the empty black screens.

The suited man threw off the designer's hand and, with a calculating glance, scrambled to the group of people who urged each other into a polite line for the transports outside.

"No. You're responsible for this."

"No more than you!" The suited man cast another apprehensive glance at her and pushed against two people to get in front of them. "Pardon, pardon," and, trained to be only quietly resentful, they moved aside.

"We have to leave, too," Connor said to Catherine.

She shook her head back and forth, back and forth. "I need to find my child. My other daughter. Victoria." She gestured vaguely at the screens.

"She with the school group?"

She nodded.

The designer picked up a collapsible tripod left behind by the broadcast crew, who had all blended into the terrified mass bunched near the exits, and folded it down with two snaps. "She's dead." She located the suited man who'd shoved his way to the head of the line and yanked a fistful of his coat to pull him backward. He fell to the floor, jumped back up.

"You stay here."

He swung wildly twice at her face, connecting the second blow to her cheek before she kicked his balls and he doubled over. "You stay here," she repeated calmly. She poked at him with the tripod as he wheezed, nudged him steadily into the shelter, shoving people aside. He tumbled down the steps into the artificial hole. The sound of his landing inside shut off the rest of his scream. She jammed the tripod into the pushbar. "It's full now," she told other people nearby who stared at her. "Get out of here, however you can."

"That was not an ethical act," Connor remarked.

"This all the transportation?" she asked spectators as they scrambled into the parking area, repeated the question in a shout which drew only a few blank backward glances as response. "You," she turned back to Connor. "How'd you get here?"

"My crew's leaving right now. Must save the equipment, you know." He gestured at a large transport van screaming out of the lot. "Oh, I guess they forgot to ask me along."

"Cold. So cold. In the meantime..." She gently shook Catherine's shoulder. "You. We'll have to get out with you. Where's the rest of your pool?"

"It was just me and the baby and my husband. And the other under-coords that came with us. They're not in our pool. I thought you knew. You were assigned, too—"

"We all have to go or die. The other girl's dead. Sorry. Your vehicle coded to you?"

Connor took Virginia from Catherine. "Let's get this one out of danger. Think of her."

Catherine blinked and looked momentarily at the sky. "It sounds like hail."

"Yeah. Heavy rain." The designer shook her arm again.

She bolted suddenly for the exit nearest the paved lot, grabbing Virginia roughly as she went.

"Wait, you idiot!" The designer pulled down two of the plastic banners hung over the dome entrance, welcoming the spectators to Site Three, flung them over the four of them as they ran outside, trying to synchronize their steps to keep the flapping shield over their heads. Catherine pressed her finger into the pad of the driver side of the plain and functional poolvan she and David had bought last year with a bonus sanction loan. Hidden locks sprang open inside their housings. She passed Virginia to Connor, who fastened her into a seat and urged softly, "Hurry." Another touch of her finger and the engine started, and she roared out of the lot, the vehicle making angry buzzes remonstrating with her for her irresponsibility. She concentrated on the steering now, put thoughts of Victoria and David away for a moment to escape the menace, the black oily smoke from the plane, the bodies lying here and there on the road....

"Where now?" she asked at the lot entrance.

"The storm was headed northwest. They usually do at first," Connor said. "It'll start turning north soon."

"That jackass Franklin. Wouldn't listen. Thought he knew it all. —Turn right. Going north's probably the only safe thing to do. But we'll have to watch. Thing is," she shouted over the buzz as Catherine drove up the highway, "once you mix neptunium and silver iodide—what a fossil; couldn't use some of the newer stuff to seed the clouds, oh, no, and neptunium's not always stable, radioactive, too, of course—and the Eutopix has this tendency to...well, bloom. Swell. Disperse. Expand. It's just a minimal hurricane. But. With the updrafts you expect in a hurricane—tornadoes... We need to put distance behind us before we stop to look for a shelter." She paused. "Sorry about your girl."

"Yeah," Connor said.

"David was in the control booth."

Connor grimaced.

A long moment passed. "So maybe somebody else should drive," the designer offered at last.

"Take too long to recode it to one of us. We'd have to stop, kill the engine; too risky," Connor objected.

The designer made a silent, wide-eyed apprehensive face for Connor's benefit. He cleared his throat. "So. Both of you know who I am. Names? Since we're all in the same fix?"

"Catherine. My baby's Virginia."

"You heard him introduce me. But nobody calls me Micaela. At the techlab I am—was 'Mike.' "

" 'Mike'?" Connor laughed mirthlessly.

"Yeah, not a dignified, responsible name. Like 'William', or 'Catherine.' " She scoffed. " 'Virginia.' 'Victoria.' I care not."

Catherine laid her forehead against the steering mechanism, and the poolvan swerved. Connor reached forward reflexively to correct the direction, and the engine died, autobrakes hissed. The vehicle slowed swiftly to a halt between electromagnetic strips designating their lane of the highway.

"God's sake, Connor, what'd you do that for?" Mike shouted. "Start it again, Catherine—get back with us."

She would like to scream. She wanted to shriek and rage and shake her fists in the air. But it was too hard to raise her head right then. So much easier to stop here. Mike screeched louder, and Connor delicately lifted Catherine's hand and pressed her forefinger into the switchlock. The engine came back to life. Dazed, she glanced at him, pressed the command for the vehicle to go forward. It accelerated steadily, fuel-efficiently.

"The regulator can't be overridden?" Mike yelled.

"Can you do this?" he asked Catherine.

She stared at the pavement and ignored the handkerchief he offered after a moment.

"Every trial you could imagine, some you couldn't," Mike gabbled on. "Tubes. Sealed rooms. In the techlab half the time it'd be the same. Nothing, and then the whole room filled up with this thick, foggy orange mess. We'd say it was breeding. Maybe it could." She shivered.

"What the hell are you talking about?"

She sucked in a quivering breath. "Clouds. Warm water. You want the clouds to warm, go up, cool off, drop the rain."

He turned in his seat to stare at her.

"Asshole Franklin. I asked for thicker glastique. No, he said; it'll hold, we don't have time to make it thicker—"

"Would you shut up?" Connor interrupted. "You didn't want to talk much, before, why now? You saw that sign on that airplane, so did I, you know that group. So they got hold of some Eutopix somehow, brought it in, that's what you're saying, now it's up there—" he pointed at the sky— "and it's falling back down on us. You got there fast. Why was that the first thing you thought of?"

She froze.

"So many other possibilities—why that one? You have something to do with it?"

"I was only responsible—"

"For the dome, yeah, you said. Well, you can't blame anybody else for *that*. That one's your baby. Better work your story out now. Get it straight. Somebody'll want it from you sooner or later. If you live to tell."

"Oh, you're making judgments? You always just read whatever got shoved under your nose. I know. I wrote some of it. You just spat it back. Some newsman."

"Where now?" Catherine interrupted.

The route north was congested, poolvans and transports backed up like miniature trains, passengers huddled inside in tense little knots. Braking lights flashed on and off as drivers tried to get closer to the vehicles ahead than the sensors would allow.

"How quick you want it to be? We could just pull over here and open the doors and wait," Mike said.

"How fast was this beast moving?"

She shrugged. "Who knows? You're one of them—you ran off the real weather people, the actual scientists, who needs 'em, right, let envireng decide, hand it over to William Connor, he'll tell us." She stopped as he looked back stonily.

"Maybe we can get some information from a broadcast. Cell's out because of the wind on the coast early this morning." He pressed buttons on the radio.

"But we have you along. Why would we need anybody else? You claimed you did all the investigation. We don't need a broadcast. Compute it in your brilliant mind."

Catherine again raised her eyes to the mirror in apprehension, looked at Virginia, who slept peacefully oblivious, her juice bottle lying next to her.

Connor stopped searching as a flat, unemotional voice filled the poolvan giving advice about the projected course of the storm, medical facilities not equipped to accept casualties, warnings against jammed escape routes.

"And here we are, right on Road 6," Mike commented. " 'Don't take Road 6. Lanes are capacity.' Guess we wait it out. Ho hum." She faked a yawn, flinched suddenly as she touched the rising bruise inflicted by Franklin. "It looked like it made people happy for a change. That's what it was supposed to do back then in the first place."

She jolted upright as the poolvan died again and Catherine

turned around. "That was my husband. My daughter. Climb in there—" she gestured at the transport in front of them— "and make your jokes." Mike pressed back against the seat and stared.

"They say it's changed directions slightly," Connor announced, listening to the broadcast. "More northerly. Sooner than expected. Not good. Start up the van again, Catherine. Start it."

He scanned the packed road ahead. "They say it's still moving thirty kilometers an hour. Fast. About twenty kilometers faster than we're going now." He pulled up his sleeve to punch at the wristcomp. "Got to leave this route. Catherine, start the engine or I'll have to get out and recode it to myself. Start it," he urged.

I hate you, her eyes told him, but she obeyed.

"Now do what I say. Sit here thirty seconds. Don't let it move."

"The sensor'll override my braking."

"Keep braking anyway."

"It'll consume the fuel."

"Keep braking."

The reluctant poolvan strained to approach the bus, pulled against the switch Catherine pressed firmly. A small distance grew between the vehicles. Electronic messages scrolled off the control panel warning them that unnecessary braking or accelerating made fuel consumption increase. Connor glanced back and forth from the empty space in front to the rear window. Billowing clouds pouring rain loomed all around them.

A few yards had opened up in front. "Catherine, don't argue, do what I say. When I tell you, pull to the right, hard, and let the braking go, and don't stop when it buzzes. —Now—" And to enforce his words, he put his hands over the back of hers, avoided touching the steering mechanism, and yanked hard, so hard she grimaced at the pressure on her skin and the mild electric warning shock. The poolvan screeched out of the marked lane and protested, the control panel blinking and a shrill hum filling the interior. With Connor's hands upon hers, she steered grimly on loose fill around the creeping vehicles and sped up the side of the highway, ignoring flashing beacons at the edge of the pavement that scolded her for being reckless.

"You're using up all the fuel," Mike commented. "So what do you have in mind for when the engine quits?"

"The fuel's going fast, Connor," Catherine agreed.

"We'll be off this road in a minute." He glanced back. Several other vehicles swerved to the right and, sheep-like, were herded back into the proper lane. "They'll never make it," he said, jerking his head at the vans and buses. "The shock scares them. A trick reporters know—overriding sensors to get somewhere fast. Takes two people, you have to ignore the electricity. Yes, very irresponsible and illegal. And you pay in fuel. That's the way these things work. You want to guzzle, it lets you; then it might leave you stranded."

"Stranded." She raised her brows.

"Your hair's on end," he said with a wry grin. "Here, right here, turn again to the right."

"The right? There's nothing to go on."

"There's a road. Or was. I grew up not far from here. It's not much more than a path now. But it doesn't go straight north. More northeast. Turn, Catherine." She winced as his hands forced the mechanism again away from its electromagnetic security. The poolvan bounced slightly on the uneven turf before its advance absorbers adjusted and smoothed the suspension. Connor guided the vehicle around a dome of earth placed as an obstacle in the old road, and suddenly they were on an ancient highway, lanes marked here and there with faded white and yellow paint. The van did not know its way now and relinquished control to Catherine, who urged it on faster, maneuvering around holes and litter. Grass grew up from the sides and in the center of the pavement; trees streaming rain leaned over them.

"I do not like this," Mike said.

"Well, it's not neat. It's rough. But it's a road I used to know, and we're going away from all that behind us."

"I don't like this. It's like going back a hundred years," she complained.

"Why don't you get out and wait for something you're familiar with?"

"Connor."

He turned away from Mike at the alarm in Catherine's voice.

"The fuel. It's almost gone." She gestured to the readout on the panel.

He shrugged. "Enough for four kilometers?"

She studied the numbers that steadily decreased. "Maybe."

He took a breath, looked backward again. "If you're religious, start praying."

"What will four kilometers get us?"

"It'll get us to a fuel supply stop, next junction of residential zoning and the highway. I know it. We can purchase more. As long as we stay away from the main roads, we won't get punished for going too fast—the sensors won't be operative. Which means we can choose the best way."

Catherine watched the numbers and slowed down to conserve the remaining fuel. Connor, understanding her decision, observed the road closely and pointed to the right or left to warn silently of hazards. A few moments passed. They neared a place where the roadside was more trimmed, and another dome of earth loomed ahead of them. "Up there," Connor said, nodding at a weathered building a few hundred meters away, and placed his hands on Catherine's again to force the poolvan back across strips waiting on the other side of the earthen hill. She clenched her teeth, consumed the last fuel with a sudden burst of speed to whirl around the dome and bounce onto the official route. The engine died, the automatic brakes applied themselves, and the poolvan stopped.

"What now?" Mike said. "We're not close enough."

In the stillness of the vehicle, they watched the windows run with rivulets and streams of rain, and they heard the wind, a howling, whistling, protest.

"One of you design people ought to invent a windshield-blower that operated with the power off," Connor said. "Can't see a thing." He reached for the manual override to lower the glass on his door.

"Don't do that!" Mike screamed. "You don't know what you could be letting in!"

"It's not close enough yet. May have washed out already, anyway." He leaned out and gestured at the figure of someone standing in the doorway of the dilapidated building. "Good." He raised the glass again. "I'd hoped. That's Thomas. He's always operated this fuel stop."

"He going to run a line over here to us?" Mike said in disbelief.

"No. I'm going to use Virginia's juice container here to get enough fuel to carry the poolvan over there. And then we can finish fueling, and leave. Do you have a better plan, Micaela?" he yelled. She leaned back in one smooth movement.

"Catherine. The lid. I'll have to hurry." He opened the door to race through the fury of the storm, becoming instantly an indistinguishable part of the gray landscape.

"Fool. *Diabhalta.*"

"Do not say that. Do not." Catherine rose part of the way from her seat and turned to face Mike. "I'll throw you out. Like you did to that, that Franklin man. Leave you right here, beside the road. Do not say that."

Mike gazed at her, took a breath to speak.

"Shut up. Don't say anything."

They sat staring at each other until Connor materialized at the door, opened it and threw himself down on the seat, his tailored suit and neat haircut dark with rain and bits of leaves.

"Well?" Mike demanded, keeping watchful eyes on Catherine.

"Let me get my breath. Hold this." He brandished the juice bottle, filled now with clear fluid. Catherine watched his face, how he had not looked at them.

"What's wrong?"

He shuddered and wiped water from his face. "He gave me this much. Gave me. Remembered me from—well, a long time ago, when I was young. But it was all he could give, just give…"

"So? Use your sanction account, Catherine," she urged. "Put the damned stuff in, Connor, and let's drive over there and get the rest."

He shook his head. "Thomas doesn't do business with me that way. It's a principle of his. Won't take sanction accounts."

"A 'principle,' that he won't do things legally? Really? What kind of criminal is he? What does he want? A trade?" She laughed in scorn. "Beads? Sex?"

"He wants currency."

Mike stared for a moment before bursting into laughter again. "Of course, what else. One of your acquaintances. He'd be somebody dealing unreported consumption. So what does he do, for his life account? How does he get his food and clothes?"

Connor threw the door open, stepped out to pour the liquid into the fuel reservoir. Catherine silently handed him his handkerchief when he flung himself back inside. He wiped his face. "It's got ten minutes on us. Better get going."

She pressed the buttons, wincing as Virginia awoke with a howl at the renewed hum of the engine.

"I'm curious, Connor. How is it there's a fuel stop that can *legally* take currency? One that doesn't do sanction account? Hmm?" In the stubborn hunch of his shoulders she interpreted the answer. "How does he even have fuel? He can't get it legitimately. Not if he takes currency. Envireng wouldn't supply him. So if he's such a good friend of yours, why doesn't he take your account, the ethical way?"

Connor turned away.

"A common criminal. That's all. Why don't you do a report on *him*?"

"Thomas gets the fuel—" He interrupted himself. "I don't know where he gets it. Officially, he doesn't. Officially, his storage tanks are empty. He's only sanctioned to analyze and repair energy packs. So. So he has to have currency for the fuel. That way it never shows up. And if we get out of this disaster, which you helped make, it's something you never knew," he added menacingly.

A soft, derisive noise escaped her.

"Because, consider, it's the only way you'll get out."

She mumbled numbers and said, "Currency. We'll just have to go somewhere that does take accounts. How far can we go on what he gave us, Catherine?"

She read the numbers and began, "Not far enough—" and stopped, remembering the jingle in her pocket. "How much would he require for unreported, Connor?"

"What?" Mike laughed again.

"Nothing extra. He just has to get it in currency."

"What docs he do with it? What could he possibly—"

"He's old, Mike! He's a collector."

"So he buys it at auctions, like the rest of them."

"No, he tries to get it this way. Earn it, he says. He's just an independent old man."

"Illegal. Criminal."

"What'd they do to him if they caught him? Nothing. He's too old. He's got this amazing collection. —So I've heard," Connor added quickly.

"I have some," Catherine said.

"Where'd *you* get currency?"

"Too long a story right now. But I've got some. With me, even. And it's truly antique. He'll like it. Enough to get us up the road. Surely we can find something there. Are we near a town?"

"Columbia. We're going to have to stop there."

"Why?"

He mouthed a few words but said nothing.

"Good stopping place. Shelter," Mike supplied. "Had no idea we were close. All those backroads made me think we'd gone further."

Catherine noted Connor's silence. He pointed ahead, and she steered the poolvan to the fuel stop, where she saw the old man waiting for them. She edged the vehicle into the repair cubicle and rummaged in her coat pocket. Glancing at Mike, she took Connor's hand and turned it palm up to lay coins in it, placing each one solemnly, remembering the circumstances of having been given it.

Mike looked at her with a sardonic smile curving her lips. "What else do you have up there?"

"You deal with him," Catherine said.

Connor closed his fist on the currency. As his door swung open again, they heard the roar of the wind and the hiss of the rain outside and looked reflexively out the back window.

"It's closer," Mike said, the amusement gone from her voice. "If it's closer, it's gotten larger, or else it's turning again. I wish he would hurry."

Latitude N 34.8
Longitude W 78.4
Wind Speed 74 knots

i

THE FUEL stop was an ancient place, a concrete and board cave where cobwebs adorned the corners and dust gilded anything left horizontal for too long. In museums Catherine had seen dioramas like this, depictions of scenes centuries ago: the aged mechanical cash register, faded cans that once might have held mysterious oils and fluids lining the upper shelves that seemed to vanish into haze in the inadequate lighting. Here was a life-size diorama, a Wonderland shop where things appeared too distant and hazy to focus on.

"Oh, my God, he's brought us to one of those replica tour stops," Mike mumbled. Catherine, glancing at her, started to agree, when the old man lifted a panel that had concealed modern fueling equipment, which he fumbled with a moment or two. As Connor passed—surreptitiously, Catherine thought—the currency to the old man and began to fuel the van, Mike's face twisted in sardonic amusement again.

Thomas stroked the coins gently, as if they were religious icons. Catherine bounced Virginia in an effort to pacify her. And they waited.

The process seemed to take far too long. Thomas said things to Connor which they could not hear, things that made both men smile and even laugh once; and then, with another look at the coins in his hand, another caress with his fingers, Thomas scowled and motioned at the sky. Gesturing at the highway and the horizon, the two men discussed something, and Thomas finally shook his head, laughing.

Connor lifted the hood of the van. In a moment, he had closed it back and opened Catherine's door.

"Over." He motioned for her to slide to the other side.

"Why?" she asked, startled.

"I've recoded with myself as driver. It'll be better if I handle this for a while."

"You can't recode unless I enter my yield number. It's not

possible. What did you do?"

"It's possible." He shrugged.

"Another trick of you broadcast types, I suppose," Mike said. "Ethical, legal types, you guys. I get more impressed with you the further we go."

Connor was silent. Catherine moved Virginia into a harness in the back beside Mike and watched Connor until Thomas approached her side window. Connor jerked his head in a nod.

"He tells me you drove in on the old route. Guts. This—" He brandished the coins closed inside his fist. "You sure you willing to give 'em up?"

She nodded reluctantly.

A slow grin broadened his mouth, a space where a tooth was missing. "Guts."

"Why don't you come up the road with us to the college?" Connor asked. "There'll be space in the shelter."

"Got a storm cellar—" he motioned outside. "I'll be all right. Anyway, I'm just about at the age. If I'm not all right, who'd care?"

"I wish you'd come."

Catherine heard Mike cough a little behind her.

"I'm heading down into the cellar right now, Willie. I choose to ride it out there."

"We have to go on, Thomas. Once more I ask—"

But the wiry old man laughed shrilly and waved a bony hand at them before turning to open the door of the repair cubicle. Connor stared pensively at him.

"Connor?" Catherine said.

"We'd better stay on the back road until we get closer; no regulating strips there."

"And so, so picturesque," Mike put in.

He opened his mouth to say something, but didn't. Catherine turned around to watch through the rear window as Thomas secured the doors of the fuel stop, his clothing whipping around like old leaves hanging on an autumn-struck tree. The scouring rain soon obscured that view, and Catherine watched the road in front now. Connor drove moderately fast, avoiding the hazards that had presented themselves on the abandoned road. They crossed streams unchanneled and untamed, raging, frothing out of their banks, spilling out onto the saturated land. Connor slowed the first several times he came to those bridges still marked with thin, rusty rectangular signs that had been painted white and yellow long ago. The first time, Catherine had glanced questioningly at him, wondering if he doubted the safety of the old bridges. He watched the tumbling water; and she felt the engine speed up when the stream was behind them, and ignored the pauses from then on.

"We didn't really need this much rain," she ventured.

"Why do you people always want to fool around with these beasts, Mike?"

"Stop calling it that. Just stop. It's not alive, it's not a 'beast.' Whatever gave you the idea of saying that? Like it's your trademark or something? And I didn't have anything to do with it. I did the dome—I was supposed to get numbers, projections, design the best shape and thickness of the glastique shelters, supervise—that was my part. I only did my part."

"Didn't do it very well. It kind of broke."

"They gave us a week and a half."

"I'll quit calling it a 'beast' when you stop saying 'the thing is.' I'm tired of that, too. Get a vocabulary."

There was a long moment of silent hostility.

"Are we more or less out of danger?" Catherine asked. "Can't we get somewhere safe, try to find out about the people back there—"

Connor touched the receiver buttons.

—unusually active in terms of tornado potential. It is possible though unlikely that the additional enhanced iodide may be producing a strengthening effect on the storm, which has started its expected curve northward and is bearing down on the town of Columbia.

"*Dul go h-olc ort,*" Mike breathed.

Severe injury should be expected upon exposure to any precipitation from this storm for some days. Casualties at the detonation site run high, with near one hundred percent mortality—

A sideward glance at Catherine, and Connor touched the buttons and silenced the voice. "We know it's following us. That's enough."

She sat as a statue, ignoring Virginia's quiet babble.

"We need to get to a safe place, think about other things later."

The vehicle sped up the road, swerving around small pools of rain and long-neglected potholes, buffeted by sudden blasts of the angry storm.

"So, Mike—what'll this do to the environment?" Connor asked in a pleasant voice.

"You don't want to know," she said grimly. "Actually, we don't know anyway. Almost every trial, they had something a little different a long time ago, half a century—"

"An eon," Connor agreed sardonically.

"It's a long time ago for me; maybe not for you. Maybe you're nearer the age than I thought." Mike continued as Connor remained quiet, "They learned then, when they used it in the subsistence drought, they learned it could change. It was supposed to be such a harmless little molecule. Really," she insisted as Connor grunted derisively. "But expose it to some compounds, or lots of electricity, lots of water, the base elements ionize. Molecules break apart." Her voice rose. "So they pulled it after all those people died. Stored it in some high-security vault. So many subversives trying to get away to Canada, wanting to make a statement as they go—you know how it is—"

Catherine's shoulders jerked involuntarily. "I do not."

"I didn't mean you personally.... Envireng's always worried somebody might try to use it again."

"Insurgent activity?"

"Yeah, Newsman. And somebody did, looks like. Right? Got hold of some, shoved it into that plane…"

"How'd they get it?"

"How does anybody get things these days? It was a little at a time. Then sold unreported. Probably. Just like your old pal back there. You know how things go missing. You already told us yourself how you get around the regs."

It seemed Connor didn't like that answer; his scowl deepened. "I still want to know why you immediately said it was that particular chemical. You didn't even act surprised. And how is it envireng let anybody mess around with it, not having its structure, chemistry, nailed down—" his hand flailed as if trying to grasp at elusive floating answers.

"Yeah, well, you mess around with it to figure all that out. That's what scientists did. Then that accident, and all of a sudden, no, let's have the government do it, they can issue regs about it. Your, your person, your David…" she narrowed her eyes, looked sideways at Catherine. "He didn't really do things, did he—more of just a tech guy, whatever they told him to do, no decisions himself? —Don't get riled up; I know he probably had to."

"You talk too much," Catherine interrupted, turning in the seat. "I didn't ask you to come with us today. It was because of regulations. David and I—" she paused, frozen suddenly at using, at actually speaking, his name— "we got this poolvan by agreeing to transport people like you in it whenever they required us to. But I didn't want you along."

Mike edged closer to the driver's seat and punched a finger in Connor's shoulder. "Go faster. Does this backroad go through all the way? Or do you know?"

"Used to." He shrugged. The answer displeased Mike, who leaned back, a skeptical frown on her face. Catherine, still turned halfway in her front seat, still glaring at Mike, thought suddenly of Victoria, sitting next to Virginia as they went shopping in the hard-earned vehicle. Victoria had that expression, the one that asked her and David why she had to take the rear all the time.

In spite of the tailored uniform she wore, Mike seemed so young.

"When we stop, you take the front," Catherine told her, wondering in the same moment why she'd blurted that out. "If you'd like."

"I'm fine here."

"I made Victoria go there today. I did." It was another almost involuntary declaration, wrung from her as she saw this young woman next to Virginia, in the place Victoria would be.

Mike grimaced. "We don't need to talk about that."

"She didn't like the school. They'd been working on this long research project, the chemistry module. Research the rain boosters, environmental requirements. She didn't like it. Didn't want to be there today. I thought about letting her stay home...."

"That was where she was assigned, and that was that," Mike remarked. "She should've felt privileged to be there—all the upper-quadrant kids. Special attention. Special supplies. How many other kids get free professional-quality compcorders, standard issue?"

Catherine clenched her fists briefly. "That was kind of her point. Why should she have one, specially—"

"Because that's the way it is."

"You see it that way? She didn't. She didn't want to be there. I made her go. Me. I made her. I'm responsible for what happened to her."

Connor glanced sideways as her voice rose. "I understand, but you have to put it off for a while."

The poolvan rolled along with jolts and bounces, the advance absorbers attempting to compensate for litter that now blew off trees in front of them and added to the ancient debris already on the pavement. Virginia nodded off again, and in the silence Catherine gazed out her window, looking down occasionally at the tiny side mirror. Bands of clouds traced across the sky behind them like heavy ink lines drawn on wet paper. She saw David's face—

"I wonder how it...if it was painful, or if—"

"It was formulated to have a very long shelf life, Catherine, and not to break down until it came into contact with the specific oil and chemistry of human skin. But they found out it expands, disperses, whatever—you get my point," she raised her brows— "even inside the human cell, so it bursts vessels. Breaks cell walls. But on the other hand, the general theory always was, even if it changed again, it wasn't especially painful. Just a theory. You want to know more about what happened, you could listen to the broadcast again."

"No."

Mike settled back at the single syllable, satisfied that she'd wrung quiet from Catherine.

The strained silence of the van conjured those last images of David again, his mouth loose with terrible peace, thin red lines streaming from his eyes and nose and mouth— The image sprang up specter-like, and she clutched her arms close and shivered.

"Don't think about it," Connor warned.

"In the old days, they'd post warnings about hurricanes. People would flock away from them like birds migrating. No designated shelters. That's what we're doing...just flocking away."

Mike sighed heavily and tapped her foot on the floor.

"My parents said the roads would be packed. Vehicles, traffic, lined up for miles. Wasting fuel. They'd go inland, far as it took to reach safety...but some stayed in spite of the warnings, tried to ride it out..."

"Fools," Mike offered, her face turned away.

"Like Thomas," Catherine added. "Riding it out."

Mike leaned forward suddenly and tapped her on the shoulder over and over, as she had Connor. "Just stop, stop it. I wish I'd been assigned another way to get there today, and could've left that grandstand with somebody else. But I didn't. So we're all together. But we don't have to chatter like we're trying to keep each other company, because we aren't. We just have to get to someplace safe. —Or just give up here. Either way, we don't have to talk."

"It's her vehicle, you selfish, arrogant twit."

"Arrogant? You know what happens if I do get out alive? I might as well die now. Everybody else at that dome already did. There aren't many others for them to hold responsible for it anymore."

"Victoria had got this habit lately of saying '*diabhalta*,' Mike," Catherine blurted. "That and other things. *Galar an bháis ort.* Everybody, everything she had no use for. *Diabhalta.* I got so tired of it. You know why I had the coins in my pocket? My father gave them to me; his father gave them to him, maybe his, before that. It was antique. My grandfather had one of those notions people get around the age—he told me to keep it on me all the time. Never know when you might use it. What if you need something, there's no electronic readers? As if there'd be something legal I'd want to buy with currency. Pat my pockets when I was around him, to check, see if I'd listened. So I humored him. I kept it." She paused. "So I could remember them."

Mike turned away again after a moment. The poolvan rattled on as the pavement gradually narrowed, and vegetation nibbled at its sides. The rain had become a torrent which even the strongest setting of the blower could not handle. Catherine stared forward to help Connor identify and avoid the obstacles, as he'd helped her earlier, when suddenly an object loomed. She spoke in a whisper: "Where're we going now?"

He too stared at the thing and slowed down. The van rumbled to a halt behind a mountain of dirt blocking the gash where a river flowed now wild and foamy and old pilings described a long-dismantled bridge.

"Nowhere," he said calmly.

ii

MIKE OFFERED an opinion of how many cubic meters of earth blocked their way to the nonexistent crossing. Connor suggested, with irony, that he'd tell the van to speed up and fly over the gap in a jump.

"We have to backtrack," he said at last.

"We can't backtrack," Mike said.

"We can't go *that* way." He gestured ahead.

"But—!" She gestured, and they were reminded of the roar of the wind.

"We can't get out and walk," Catherine said.

Connor glared at the mountain, then abruptly pressed buttons and whirled the vehicle around to drive south.

"This's crazy!" Mike screamed.

"Other roads turn off this one. Didn't you notice? Here and there. They run in the general direction of the electromag highway. We'll find one, turn west, get back on it. There's no other way."

"West?" Mike yelled. "We'll cross the path of the storm for sure then!"

"West. Get on the highway, we're actually close to Columbia—"

"Why not east? Head away from it. Forget Columbia. All those people are gonna die anyway— Let me drive, Connor. You're not thinking straight."

"Okay, Mike, you want to stop, you want to get out and recode it, here—do it—"

"Why do we have to go to Columbia?" Catherine asked as the poolvan flew down the road, Connor now no longer attempting to evade the debris. "The fuel's going fast at this speed," she warned, her eyes on the readout panel.

"My mother and father are in Columbia," he said. "I'm taking them with us, to their shelter there."

"They're probably already in one, Connor. Forget them, turn east—"

"I'm going to make sure."

"*Diabhalta.*" With the softly breathed curse, Mike shuddered and crossed herself, and, seeing the gesture, Connor rolled his eyes.

The looming sky was now in front of them, blooming and billowing, lit up and bleached with blasts of occasional lightning.

Connor drove grimly, glancing back and forth from the pavement to the readout, but Mike and Catherine stared mesmerized at the horizon. The van slowed. Catherine sucked in her breath and looked at the fuel estimation, then at Connor, who squinted and peered through the streams of wind-driven rain creeping across the window.

"Here...somewhere, here..."

He swerved the van to the right, and they were suddenly on a muddy, unpaved road as he fought for control and Mike shrieked in the back.

"Hang on. It's not that long. As I recall. No bridges. Just little wash-throughs..."

The overhanging clouds dipped lower. They were surrounded by pelting rain.

"A few more kilometers," Connor muttered.

The muddy road ended before it intersected with the electromag highway, another small dome to be skidded around and bypassed, a scream of the warning buzz inside and Connor's hair suddenly lifted in spikes around his head at the mild shock. And then they were on the highway again, accompanied by a few vehicles, all racing northward, all of whose passengers seemed mesmerized by the rain sliding down one window or another.

"Where are the vans? The buses?" Mike asked. "It was end-to-end when we left."

"That was about twenty-nine kilometers back," Connor said. "They didn't move fast enough. The ventilation system sucked in the air." He shrugged and sighed, and Mike turned her head to the window.

iii

COLUMBIA HAD a certain relationship with its university: So long as the students abided by the contracts they signed on admission—so long as there was general peace and not too much antagonism directed at envireng—the town honored all the sanction loans and accounts, even when they were maxed. Envireng's problems with the students were envireng's problems. Occasional sweeps, followed by the permanent absence of some students and silence of campus authority, were not Columbia's business. Now that the storm was behind them again, Mike calmed a little.

"I enjoyed this place. Got my degree here," she told them. Connor and Catherine asked no questions, and she went silent. Virginia awoke, fretting and plucking at the harness; this brought Catherine out of her nightmare reverie with a sudden shiver.

"She's hungry. Let me dash into a shop, anyplace still open, get something for her, before we check on your parents."

Connor signaled the van to decelerate. The readout gently questioned the need for this, as the speed limit posted in the electronic strips had not changed; and, suddenly annoyed, he punched in the command with hard taps on the panel.

"She's hungry," Catherine said again, shrinking back from the anger on his face. "Haven't we made up a few minutes by now?"

He waved his hand dismissively and said nothing, looked right and left before steering neatly into a slot beside a store that would seem to have dairy products and bread. Many people rushed in and out; a man wearing a shirt appliqued with the store's name stood outside the front windows, spraying them with an opaque liquid that squirted from a long cylinder he swung in his left hand.

"Try not to be long; I have to make the other stop, too; and it seems they're shutting down—" He spoke brusquely, looked straight ahead; not at her. She got out, turned back and lifted Virginia.

"Give her a rest from the van," she explained disingenuously, holding back other words at the sight of Connor's set face and staring eyes.

The store was full of people picking up items and rushing to terminals to slip their account strips through the readers. A soft electric hum buzzed in Catherine's ears—the nonstop buzz of cleared authorizations. She elbowed past people, Virginia turning around and around, curious about the polite, quiet, frantic purchases taking place. Grampa would be out of his depth here today, Catherine thought. All sanction transfers here; no self-respecting consumer would show up with currency. And all food accounts were honored, with overdrafts automatically subtracted from fuel allowances. Nobody went hungry any more, as they had at the time of the subsistence drought. A liter of milk, some juice; crackers and bread... The stock cubicles were stripped almost bare today. She found a sealed bag of preserved fruit pieces, a box of cereal, and, recalling Connor's words, ran with them to the reader at the end of the last row, trying to remember whether she and

David had maxxed their sanction allotment for the month and would have it debited to fuel. The three people ahead of her drew their strips through the slots—zip! zip! zip!—as if they were razor cutters opening cartons, then raced outside, their purchases swinging back and forth in bright-colored bags bearing the name of the store. On her way out Catherine passed the owner hurrying back inside; the door behind her hissed shut, and he began making an announcement over his address microphone.

The poolvan was nowhere in sight.

Somehow she'd known it would be that way. It was why she'd taken Virginia. She stood frozen under the glastique canopy, the baby babbling and pulling on the sack that dangled from Catherine's right arm. Fool to have allowed Connor to recode the van to himself. Fool to have gone into the store and left the other two alone and in control of the vehicle.

"Beek!" Virginia called, leaning down toward the sack.

"In a minute, Gin—" She closed her eyes, sick with responsibility, feeling bodies bump into her as they fled to buses and other vans, hearing their courteous pardon-me's and, above all, the just-unpleasant-enough-not-to-be-ignored clatter and buzz of the public warning system. David should be here to know where the closest designated shelter was; he would know things like that. She looked around. She would lie down over there beside the store, away from the whipping wind and pouring rain; she would hold Virginia close in her arms and wait for whatever was in the orange sky. She would open the juice and offer bread, and they would have a picnic before they died in that peaceful, bloody moment when the microscopic pellets dissolved upon their skin. Gently pushing her way through the urgent multitude, she found the alleyway on the north side of the building and leaned against the wall.

"Beek!" Virginia demanded.

She slid downward, her back to the plaster, her knees bending as she sat on paved walkway. Virginia flopped on her middle as if in a saddle and eyed the sack hungrily. She kissed the child's forehead and opened the juice bottle with shaking hands, tore the bread wrapper. It would have been wiser to keep the containers intact, the better to reseal them and hoard them in the shelter, but there would probably be no shelter now, and Virginia was hungry. Rain ran furiously down carefully-planned gutters at her feet and made a noise-deafening curtain separating them from the crowds that raced up the walkways.

Virginia ate the bread greedily, slurped from the juice bottle, spilling it down the front of her clothing as it poured from an opening too large for her to manage. Remembering the little bottle Connor had used for the fuel, Catherine closed her eyes and shuddered with anger and bitterness. Virginia watched curiously and ate the bread.

They'd planned that excursion to the beach for after the storm. *We've seen sunsets*, David scoffed. *You can see sunsets anywhere. But the ocean'll be great, awesome, the weather'll be clear—it's always that way after a storm*. It was almost embarrassingly consumptive, she'd told him; but he'd get a bonus for his work—"A happy bonus!" he'd laughed. And when she asked again how they could afford it, he reminded her they'd been frugal for so long. Arrangements were made with the administrator at Victoria's school, who disapproved but would not argue with an under-coord who'd lately received a lot of positive publicity. And Victoria'd been grateful enough to be released from attendance that she'd allowed herself some interest in the excursion.

Virginia ate bits of bread and slurped less voraciously now, the first gnawing of hunger gone. Catherine gazed at the grey curtain in front of them, watched the folds in it shift as the wind howled. Victoria had always hated the upper-quadrant school. It was a choice, but like so many of the choices, one with an edge: If she didn't attend that center, her fees at any other one wouldn't be deferred. She'd been so uncooperative at first that David at last had to threaten not to let the friends she had from the third- and even second-quadrant schools visit her. When she went to their houses without permission, he'd been amused; he overlooked that violation of rules and compromised by having her carry the pager. Sometimes she'd respond when they transmitted signals to her, and sometimes she wouldn't. We don't know where she may be or what she might be up to with those kids, Catherine complained—they could be roaming the countryside, hooking up with the insurgents, buying unreported... With what? David asked calmly. How could they buy anything unreported without currency? She knows ethics and responsibility.

Victoria'd been embarrassed when they earned the van. None of her lower-quadrant friends' parents owned vans. She refused to travel certain places in it with them.

And then there was the uproar about her compcorder, security-coded by her in a way that even the instructors couldn't get through, and she refused to open it, facing down the master, her dark hair framing her face, defying them. David had laughed about that later, too, but had to seem stern and threaten privileges as punishment, and yet envireng sent them commendations about their bright daughter, as if envireng were unconcerned about rebelliousness, or perhaps even valued it. She brought home errorless work and flung it at them, and she told them, "If I keep it up, they'll let me have dismissal in one less year, and I'll be at university and away from here." Then she came home one day with the dark hair bleached colorless.

The image of David in the booth appeared again on the shifting grey curtain. She shivered and shook her head to make the picture go away, began to close the package of bread and reseal the juice. She could not lie down and die. Virginia deserved more, at least an effort. She tied all the food up in the sack and, slinging it over her right shoulder, hauled the baby up to hold her face close to her chest. Huddling next to the wall, she edged to the storefront under the glastique canopy. Whichever way people were hurrying was where the shelter would be, surely. She'd follow them. Someone yanked her by the arm on which the sack hung, and she grabbed it back protectively. No one would get what she'd bought.

"You idiot! Where've you been?"

She was furious, and overwhelmed with relief, at Connor's loud demand, his face grim with frustration and maybe something else as he pulled her up the sidewalk in a trot.

"The van wasn't here when I came out. I figured you'd gone on, left us—"

He thrust her into the vehicle, sped around to the driver's side and mashed buttons in silence. She turned to find Mike white-faced behind them as the van roared up the street, the readout protesting politely about fuel consumption. She buckled Virginia into a seat. Connor yanked the steering one way and another, turning down streets and avenues under new-growth pines and oaks planted during the last decade. The sky was dark, a heavy, constant downpour of rain falling, and the howling of the wind the only sound in the poolvan.

"Did you find out anything about the projected path?" she

asked.

"No."

Mike stared ahead, her body convulsed occasionally in a brief, intense shiver.

"Where's your parents' house?"

"A block away." He said no more, and she stayed quiet herself but watched him, a resolution forming. He stopped in front of a row of stackhouses, new saplings planted in front that bent double now in the gale. The apartments stood four high, with nothing much to distinguish one from another, plain and functional. The parking lot was almost deserted.

"Recode my van back to me," she said. "Before we leave, put it back to me."

He turned a look of contempt on her, taking away her courage for a moment, then edged the vehicle under the shelter stop and ordered it to shut itself off.

"You want to find the roads, fine. We'd all be dead, at that hump of dirt, if I weren't here."

She gripped his arm. "You only have to tell me where to go. You don't have to do the driving. Making the decisions. Taking them from me."

"Fine, your first choice, then: Sit here in your van. Or come in if you please. There's a basement where all the occupants go for social gatherings. Safer than staying in the van. But your choice. We won't be long."

She hadn't let go of his arm, shook it now, pushed her face near his. "I'll go with you. You recode my van after." He turned away.

They scrambled out, Mike breathing hard behind them.

There was a glazed certificate posted conspicuously on the wall by the front door inside the enclosed loggia. " 'Compulsory research contract'?" Catherine read aloud. "You didn't say they were at the age."

"Three years plus, actually. —After you, *ladies*," he said with irony directed at Mike, who panted heavily as Connor opened the door using his own code and they crossed the threshold. The sarcasm seemed lost on her.

iv

CATHERINE HADN'T ever actually known anyone under compulsory research contract. Not that it was something you only used a hushed voice when you mentioned it—unreported elder medication or food, things like that; there was plenty of information, available to everybody, it being the end-will decision everybody eventually had to make.

But there were no elder stackhouses in her neighborhood, only family habitations; she and David had not chosen living quarters near one of the clusters. Economics determined where the patients lived; research was easier when people were grouped, travel simpler, expenses lower, if ten lived in a small area and could be monitored together.

For half a century everybody'd had the right to determine their lifespan, within envireng frameworks, and that meant every immediate physical need, housing, food, was provided, to the age. It was humane, rational. The old way of letting those with resources consume all the end-will health care, leaving everybody else to die in poverty, wasn't right. It was one thing that caused the rioting during the subsistence drought.

The house smelled like fresh antiseptic, but not quite.

Connor gestured in the direction of a room behind the front sitting area, a room with dim lighting and a calm electronic voice droning. In Catherine's arms Virginia peered at the spare furnishings: a thin screen on one wall; a table holding an assortment of seashells and an oval electronic relay for transmitting data; incongruously, three broadcasting awards— "Investigative Reporting Excellence—" surrounding a framed photograph of a boy. A reclining chair on which could be hung chemfeed lines. Thin, delicate curtains over the two windows.

"Mother, Father. Pleasant day, hm."

They seemed unsurprised to see Connor, unsurprised at the tone of his voice. He patted the old woman's shoulder, made an adjustment to the pillows behind the old man's back, stepped away and focused on the broadcast. Mike stood, mouth slightly open, mesmerized by the sight of the shattered dome, scoured opaque white and blasted open like a dead barnacle. No mother-of-pearl anymore.

"Been listening to the advisories?"

Connor's father nodded. "Headed this way."

"They've reported this chemical is well integrated into the storm," the woman said, emphasizing "reported" as if she had doubts. "They say the first parts will be here in half an hour."

Mike made a soft, alarmed grunt. "Less."

"What are your plans?" Connor was serene, pulling up his sleeve, punching at the wristcomp.

The old man watched the broadcast. "Plans?"

"Getting to a shelter. You know, plans."

The long rubber tube threaded into the old man's shoulder wiggled a little. To Catherine it seemed he might be about to laugh.

"I'm not going to the shelter, crowding in with all the other pitiful cases like me, waiting out this—" he flung an obscene gesture at the screen, the one Victoria used when she thought she could get by with it.

"You aren't safe in here. It's not airtight."

"Connor, time..." Mike said.

"Here I stay."

"You're under contract. You can't do that," Connor insisted. "You have to protect the research investment. You signed to."

"Money!" The old man wiped his mouth after spitting out the word.

"And time. And effort. And results. You and Mother have to come with us."

"How is it you're here, Will?" the woman asked.

"Saw your broadcast van in a report a few minutes ago. About a couple hundred others, several transports, all stopped on some road. Cameras—close-ups. Gruesome sight—" He shuddered. "Didn't see you. We figured you'd made it out somehow."

"How're they getting the images?" Connor turned swiftly to study the screen with a technical curiosity Catherine found repulsive.

"Some kind of gas masks, moon suits. Hovered overhead, then got 'em out pretty damn quick. Stay a while, they'll broadcast it again." The old man snickered.

"Connor, time—" Mike fidgeted.

"These people—" he gestured at Catherine, jerked his head insultingly toward Mike— "and I were left behind at the observation site. You tell me you saw my crew. They moved fast to save the equipment and themselves. So they thought. Some of the first to try to leave. So they got a big dose. This's Catherine, her child Virginia—" He paused, raised his brows as if waiting for a surname, which Catherine chose not to give. "Her husband was one of the undercoordinators on site."

"Oh, my dear, I'm sorry."

From the old woman's words and grimace she knew the thing she didn't want to accept yet.

"And her older daughter's class were there for the school field lab," Connor went on.

"Oh, my."

Catherine's eyes shifted momentarily again to the blasted dome. A long silence substituted for comfortless words.

"Connor," Mike said.

"Oh, yes." He waved a careless hand in her direction. "And Micaela Sánchez. You may've already heard her name a time or two."

She took a step toward him, but a sudden laugh from the old man, a deep, hearty guffaw that sent the tube that ran into a jerking dance, stopped her. "Micaela Sánchez?"

"Theo." Connor's mother laid a hand on his shoulder as if in reproach and spoke to Mike: "You know they're looking for you."

Mike went very still, dark eyes glaring, her mouth twitching just a bit at the left edge.

"Connor, recode the van. If you and your parents want to stay here, your choice, but I'm taking Virginia to the nearest shelter. Where would that be, Mrs. Connor?"

"Ruth. It's Ruth, Catherine. You're ten minutes from the closest one—"

"You two are going with us. I assume the pack's portable, and you'd be within guidelines under the circumstances. In fact," Connor went on, frowning at his father, "you'd be violating contract not to. Bring me a cover, or a wrap, Mother, and show me how to arrange the feeder line." He gingerly picked up the small chembox and dropped it into the old man's lap from which it was flung with one violent motion.

"I'm guessing there's no danger to anybody else if that thing leaked?" Connor asked in the same calm tone of voice.

"Who knows? Isn't that part of the contract, too? They take care of me, treat me, I don't get to know what it is. Maybe it poisoned you when you picked it up—" and he laughed.

"I don't think that's funny." Connor wiped his hand on his

pants.

"There's no danger, Will. I change it myself all the time."

"Then pick it up and let's get going."

"Will, we can't go—"

"Don't tell me you can't go there!" he yelled. "You have an obligation to go there. You signed a contract. I won't be helping you violate something you signed—"

"Connor, your father's not leaving with us." Catherine had sized it all up during the shouting. She knew, as Connor somehow did not. He started to say something else, paused.

"He's not going, are you, Theo?"

"No, I'm not. She's right. It's my choice this time, not yours. If I go this way, it looks like it won't be so bad. Your pardon, Catherine; I don't mean to add grief. The hell with letting *them* choose. I'm staying here. You had your say-so about it a few years ago. I'm not listening this time."

The two men glared at each other as Mike tapped a wild rhythm on the floor.

"You knew what it was, when you signed."

"Bah."

Connor swung toward the old woman. "Mother?"

"You know I stay with him. I won't leave him."

"I don't know how you recoded the van, Connor, but I want your number, now. I'm getting Virginia to that shelter. Stay or go or whatever, but give me the number."

"I'll do it myself." He spoke very quietly, every movement about him suddenly quiet, even his soft footsteps toward the front of the stackhouse. "She stays, too," he flung at Mike, whose face twisted up as if she might cry.

"That's her decision. She can go with me if she pleases."

Mike turned grateful eyes on Catherine.

"She's responsible for all those people. Your people. She should accept responsibility for it."

"But you won't put it on her. If she wants to go with me, she can."

He made a contemptuous sound and shrugged as he left the room, and in a moment they heard the roar and sizzle of the wind and rain outside the door.

"Would you reconsider?"

The old man shook his head at her in a series of jerks, almost twitches, and yanked the tubing from the square box to tie the end into a tight knot, ignoring the loud buzz that shrieked from the device.

"They'll be angry when they come to reattach it—you know how they are!" But Ruth pulled a chair near the private-care issue one he occupied and sat down.

Virginia reached for the shells on the table.

"Let her have one."

They'd intended to go to the beach.

Catherine placed a conch in the child's hand, and she turned it over and over, examining the spikes and whorls before Catherine put it to her ear. She listened, her eyes wide, at the silence.

They waited a while more, and then Connor was back.

"Well, I see you're as stubborn as you always were," he said, holding his hands over his ears. "It seems to be getting heavier. You'd better go, Catherine."

"You have to go with her, Will. I've tried to tell you, but our shelter's been full for some time. They said so in one of the broadcasts. They sealed it. You can't go there."

"Oh, God," Mike wailed softly.

Connor scoffed, turned to Ruth: "Why's it full already? Didn't they know the numbers? They always know the numbers. Well, that leaves the university. She could make it there, I imagine."

"She can't. Don't head that way. There's something going on up there again."

"Kids playing rebel. Who cares. They won't be playing for long, in this stuff."

"Do you have university clearance, Catherine?"

"I don't have a position there; David never did, we didn't have children there yet—"

"Will does. Clearance. Because of the news."

"But you said not to go there."

"Will has clearance to the ranking shelter."

"Ranking shelter?" Mike echoed. "What d'you mean, 'ranking shelter'?"

"For university officials. You couldn't get into it on your own. And with the rioting…"

"Rioting?" Mike asked. "Actual rioting?"

"Won't be much rioting. Even zealots believe in self-preservation," Connor remarked. "They'll duck into their own little holes at the last minute. They always do. I've covered some of their tantrums before."

"If you came in Catherine's van, she already risks charges of accomplice with Miss Sánchez here. And she's slowed down because you brought her here. So you have to go with her. The least you could do is get her into that shelter you have access to."

"I'll just give her the code."

"It's not your time. You'll go." She rose from the chair to pat his cheek. A small, thin woman, Catherine realized, who came up only to Connor's shoulder now at her advanced age. "This is our decision. You have responsibilities besides us right now."

"And you aren't at the age yet anyway," the old man snickered. "Are you."

"I'm leaving, Connor." Catherine shook the old man's hand, nodded at Ruth, walked through the doorway, aware of Mike following immediately behind her.

"This is wrong."

"Get out of here!" the old man shouted. Catherine turned back, alarmed at the sound of breaking glass as something shattered. Mike, her eyes glazed with fear, tentatively shoved her forward.

"Go, go, go..."

"Get out of here!"

"This is wrong! It's not right to do this!" —more thuds from things apparently tossed at the door. Mike nudged Catherine through the sitting room, through the front door which questioned who they were and demanded a finger-ID before they left, to facilitate their readmission. They ran to the van, rain washing under the shelter stop and soaking their legs to the knees. Catherine had read all the pre-releases about the storm, knew the howling meant the eye of the hurricane was somewhere near, the dead center of a conglomeration of gales and precipitation, just a storm; but it seemed a live thing now. Beast, indeed. Mike chanted, "Door, door, door—" and, bending double, threw up on the ground in one heave before flinging herself inside.

"Are you exposed?" Catherine yelled, pushing Virginia into her seat.

"No. Go."

She thrust the trembling forefinger into the switch-lock. Nothing. Had Connor tampered with the van so much it had frozen, its tangle of electronic inner guts concluding something illegal or unethical was afoot and it had chosen not to cooperate?

"Damn him!" Mike screamed.

Catherine lifted the finger, put it down again, more insistently, remembering Connor's vigorous punching of the controls before they reached his parents' home. Maybe the computer had adjusted to a heavier touch. The motor did not catch.

She started to try again, when the other front door was jerked open and then slammed shut, and Connor threw himself against the seat. He yanked her hand away and pressed his own finger into the lock. The engine immediately roared.

"Leave now. Back up. Head north—we have to go left first. Turn left here. Go."

She obeyed the orders, fury boiling in her. After they'd passed two blocks of housing and were speeding along the highway again, sensors and polite cautions scrolling across the panel, she turned furiously to him. "I told you to recode it to me!"

"You're driving, aren't you? —Right, here."

She hadn't thought of that. She turned again, the course now corrected almost to due north.

"We should go east," Mike offered.

"The storm's on us, right over us," he said. "We're almost directly in the eye. Can't you tell?"

Catherine risked a glance aside. The rain was fierce, the wind a screaming thing.

"We have to get some distance from it. I understand from a broadcast just as I—just as I was leaving, a minute ago, the chemical seems to be heavy in the rear wall of the storm. Lots of it. Drive, Catherine. We can outrun it. Turning east will only put us in the path of the bands circling from the rear. Go."

She felt her arms shaking now, a reaction to his words, or the damp. Virginia was altogether too alert, as if she understood everything they were saying. She did not want Virginia to remember this. Heeding Connor's instructions, she pressed the vehicle into more speed, to which it objected courteously with a soft little hum. Connor laughed.

"Damn things. They have too much sense for their own good. I ought to've ripped out its brain."

"How can I drive when you had to start it?"

"The startup's coded to me. Nobody else could take it from you, and just, for instance, force you to yield, because they'd never get my number from me, so they'd go nowhere. Just in case the thought crossed anybody's mind."

Catherine did not glance at Mike. "So you intended to leave all along? You never intended to stay with them?"

"I'm sorry for you. Having to share company with us, hm. A coward and a murderer."

"I'm not a murderer!" Mike shrieked.

"No, I expected them to do the right thing and come with us, Catherine. Till the very last I expected it." He shook his head.

"You never cared about their contract at all, you liar," Mike said, and turned her face to the cold window at the lack of denial from him.

Latitude N 34.9
Longitude W 78.4
Wind Speed 68 knots

CONNOR DICTATED directions out of the residential section. They went as fast as the strips would allow, mostly alone on the streets, and a terrible silence roared inside the van. Even Virginia was quiet, squirming occasionally in her harness in a way that reminded Catherine the few extra diapers she'd brought for what she'd believed would be a brief outing wouldn't be enough now for a stay in the shelter. She started to ask Mike if she had any idea how long before the Eutopix biodegraded, if it would do that, or would take to be cleaned up, if not; but Mike and Connor both sat grim, quiet, watching the sides of the road. Catherine wondered if he was thinking of Ruth and his father, and that he hadn't been kind to them in those last moments. Just as she'd be haunted by Victoria's sad, sullen face this morning. The vision materialized in front of her again, and with a gasp and another shudder she shoved it aside, eliciting a mildly questioning look from Connor before he turned away again.

She'd indulge in grief when Virginia was safe.

Envireng generally approved of, even encouraged, plastic surgery for public figures. It was a way to publicize an image of a healthy elder, so it was hard to guess how old Connor was: above fifty, perhaps, fifty-five? He might be a decade older than she. And the woman behind her, in her neat synthetic-fiber dark suit and business hair style, obviously, deliberately adding age to herself: How old could she possibly be—twenty-seven, maybe, trying to pose for forty to wring respect from an envireng bureau which had nicknamed her "Mike" in a time when nicknames carried almost the same stigma as that gesture Victoria used. She felt reluctantly sorry for her and almost blurted compassionate words, but stopped. After they were sheltered, this connection would be done. She'd distance herself from Mike from necessity, and by choice from Connor.

Something under eight kilometers separated Columbia from the university sharing its name—a distance lengthened by the imposed limit of the strips and the rain driven against the windshield.

Catherine drove past a thin metal sign jerking from side to side in the gale: They'd crossed onto campus. A gentle buzz advised her that the van's speed had been further reduced in compliance with the programmed limit here, and at the sound, Connor sighed and looked ahead. "Next intersection, go left. I'll have to direct you from there. The shelter's not marked."

"I'm sure." Mike's voice was laced with irony again. "Say, Connor, when I was studying here, I never knew about any designated shelter except the student one. So what's it for: people more important than the rest of us?"

"Here: drive into this parking lot. I'll tell you the code," he continued, ignoring Mike.

"See, the thing is, they preached at us all the time about how we were more of a democracy, after the drought. How steps were taken to see nobody got unfair advantages anymore."

"You mean, after the last time you people used your little chemical," he said grimly. "Five A seven seven six Oh. Wait for the okay," he told Catherine. "There's another sequence after that."

She pressed the keypad that offered itself beside the electronic gate.

"One C two O three N," he said. A smooth voice announced, "Cleared. Proceed."

"How long did you spend thinking up that code?" Mike sneered.

"See, *the thing is*," he mocked, turning to the woman behind him, "there's no such thing as a democracy, not that way, in that sense. Right, Catherine? Even your daughter, your Victoria, knew it, with her special privileges and little compcorder."

"All the schools get equal money," she answered, "except the second- and third-quadrant ones spend it on other priorities."

"Sure. Absolutely. All right, ladies—" again with emphasis and a jerk of the head toward Mike— "we'll be there as soon as Catherine maneuvers through this drive."

"Like a hedge maze," she grumbled, a great relief loosening the muscles of her shoulders which had trembled for so long. "Nobody'd ever guess a shelter was here."

"That's the point." Mike's voice was softly mocking.

"You know, Micaela, I was thinking, you've contributed absolutely nothing so far. Nothing. You sneered at Catherine's currency that brought you here, you sneered at this place that's going to save your ass. Yes, it's for important people in this phony democracy. Presidents, governors. Envirengs. Like you. But you won't get into this shelter, anyway, will you," he continued, shouting over her interruption.

"What do you mean?"

"You've had publicity. You've been demonized. Who's gonna want you saved?"

She sat frozen. "Nobody has to know who I am."

"Oh, they'll ask. What'll you say then?"

"I'll use some other name."

He laughed.

"You won't keep me out. I know."

"Why shouldn't we go in and leave you out? Give me a good reason. People would probably consider it justice."

She met his gaze with a cold smile. "Because it wouldn't be ethical, Connor, like you told your poor old father."

Alarmed, Catherine put out a hand to stop his lunge and then groaned. "Damn. I killed the engine again because of you two."

"No, you didn't," he said. He yanked her down to the floor as her window turned into a crazed sheet of crystals before falling inside the vehicle. Mike shrieked and threw herself prone across the seat.

"Get the baby out of the harness! Get Virginia—get her out!" Connor yelled, and Catherine, restrained by his body over hers, heard the snaps and clanks of the buckles as Mike undid them. Virginia protested loudly. Catherine twisted her head sideways to see Mike hold the child down next to her on the seat as she thrashed and wailed. The van bumped gently from side to side, and then there was a crash against the back door.

"Out! Get out!"

Catherine raised her head to look at Connor, her eyes wide and agonized.

"There's a baby in here!" he shouted.

For a moment the thuds stopped as if someone were listening to verify the source of the screams. Catherine reached backward as far as her arm would stretch; she couldn't touch Virginia. Connor laid a hand on her back to hold her down.

"Get out!"

"There's a baby with us!" Connor repeated.

"Yeah. Bring it along."

His hand under her chin, Connor turned her face to hold her eyes even with his and nodded. "Don't say any more than you can help. Let me talk. Mike, slowly, roll off the seat—don't stand up— and hold Virginia. Now. Pass her to Catherine."

The child's arms clutched Catherine's hair, her legs wrapping over her back. Mike squatted behind the front seat.

"Out!"

"We're coming! —Me first," he said in a whisper, raising himself from the floor. The women heard a soft click as he unlocked the van, and then his curse as he was pulled out. A pale, thin face framed with bleached hair thrust itself inside. Catherine scrambled up to sit with her back to the man, Virginia clasped to her chest.

"You. Out here. Then you—" he gestured at Mike. "You know what this is?"

"Yeah, you went and stole a charge gun. Very tough. We're impressed."

"You talk big. Get out." He thrust the shiny device in Mike's face. She stared at him, her mouth curved sardonically as Catherine struggled past him. Connor stood in front of four other armed youths—three men and a woman, all wearing the same kind of big coat with many pockets. Bleached-hair poked at Mike's back as she dragged along.

"So we're all getting drenched. All going to die if we don't go in," Mike said. "What're you trying to accomplish? Kill a couple of women and a man and a baby? Got a quota to meet?"

"Why're you here? How'd you have the code?" Bleached-hair demanded.

"That would be me," Connor offered.

"Stay back! So what kind of big money are you?"

"Why don't you let her take her baby inside the shelter, and the rest of us can stand out here and talk as long as you got the nerve."

"Shut up!" one of the youths near him shouted, jabbing the cylinder into Connor's stomach.

"He's that guy that does the broadcasts." The twitchy young man seemed impressed. Bleached-hair scowled.

"Listen." Mike cocked her head to one side. "Rain's changing. The center of the storm's almost here. You fools know what's on the other side?" She smiled. "Some special little chemicals, all about to fall down on your stupid little heads."

"Hey." Bleached-hair returned the bright grin, held his arms out. "Nothing's happening." The grin disappeared. "So you get wet. Nobody believes all the garbage authority's put out. What they're really doing, it's an experiment on mind control. Scare us into being sheep and running off because of wind and rain. So next time we'll do what they say even faster."

"You fools are all about conspiracies," Mike commented.

"I bet the news guy knows what's really going down."

"Everybody with any intelligence, not just me, knows to get out of the storm," Connor said.

"But it's not just the storm. They're doing another test, we know. So why're you here, investigator guy, videoing, gonna report on us?"

Remembering Connor's admonition, Catherine stayed quiet, watching the man half-strutting, half-irritated pacing back and forth in front of them. His companions, for all their bravado, glanced nervously upward every few moments.

"Shelter in Columbia's full," Mike offered. "He's got access to this one. We have a baby to protect."

He glanced at Virginia. "A reg baby. You ask permission to get her?" Smirking, he thrust his face near Catherine's and then whirled around, and rain slung off the wispy colorless locks of hair into their eyes. "We want those in there," a jerking motion toward the steel shelter door, "we want them out. They're no different from anybody else. We knew there was another shelter; tonight we found it. We were all discussing it when you arrived. Here, Newsman." He shoved Connor beneath the overhang in front of the sealed door. "And I get the baby." He reached for Virginia.

"She's just a year old!"

He shook his head back and forth, again pushing his face into Catherine's. "I don't care how old she is. We're all worth the same thing to them—nothing. She's nothing to me. She goes with the newsman. She needs to cry."

Catherine glanced at Connor and caught his slight nod. Bleached-hair took the baby and held her out at arm's length; the rain soaked her head and face, and she shrieked louder. He laughed, brought her near the overhang, stood still in the storm so that they were drenched.

"No, big-talker." He prodded Mike with the charge gun. "You cool off for a while in the weather." She stepped backward and kept a scornful smile turned on him as the rain and wind gradually reduced her business coiffure to a dripping black helmet. The other commandos watched and fidgeted.

"Tell them there's a baby that'll die if they don't open the door, Newsman." Holding Virginia now against him with one hand, he fumbled in the pocket of his oversized coat and tossed a small voice amplifier to Connor, which the broadcaster held against the steel door.

"Now, kid, scream away," Bleached-hair told Virginia. He jostled her to elicit a wail and turned to laugh at Catherine.

"They're threatening this child's life," Connor said calmly into the amplifier.

"Who are you? Who's talking?" a voice boomed metallically from a speaker over the door.

"William Connor. Broadcaster. We came here because other shelters were closed. This group took control of our vehicle, took the baby, the child—"

"Wait a minute," one of the other youths said. "I know you—"

Mike jumped a little, the sardonic smile frozen. "Not likely. I don't mingle in your circles."

"I know you," he insisted. "You were a student here last year. I know. Hey, Richard—" He pointed his cylinder at her. "She was here last year."

Bleached-hair shoved Virginia onto Connor and, splashing through two inches of water, planted himself in front of Mike. "What's your name?"

"What part of your rotten brain would make you think I'd tell you?"

He grasped her face roughly, twisted it sideways, his fingers digging into her cheek. She flinched but said nothing.

"But I would appreciate it. I see you already have a nice little bruise." He massaged the knot with his thumb. "A few more would make you symmetrical. What's your name?"

"She's that Sánchez," the woman said, eyeing her, "that one they keep mentioning in the updates. She was here last year. I remember seeing her pictures in the media. All your little awards. You used to be with us!" She approached, turned her head sideways to confirm the identification.

"Look close. Be sure," Bleached-hair said, jerking Mike's face right and left.

"You were one of us!" She swung the shiny weapon against Mike's back. "Traitor!"

"We can't help you. The door's sealed," the metallic voice blasted again, echoing as if in a cavern. The students turned as one toward the shelter door; Bleached-hair cursed and trod furiously back to Connor.

"Rain's stopped!" Mike announced.

Bleached-hair laughed, gazed upward at the first glimpse of a hole in the clouds through which a patch of distant clear blue tantalized them before being veiled again. He took the voice amplifier from Connor and screamed into it, "You in there! Baby goes first! And we got one of your envirengs. She'll be last."

"I'm not an envireng—" Mike began.

"You can decide: Which ones in between? We'll be coming in soon. Be choosing," he taunted. "Get the van's computer," he ordered, turning from the door.

The woman fished a tool from a pocket. Catherine watched in anguish as the vehicle's hood rose, water rushing down its surface, and the van's inner brain was removed with a few deft twists of the tool and a sudden yank.

"All right. Detonator pack— See, we know how to design things, too," he advised Mike with a hard slap on her face. He tossed the charge gun to one of the other students, the woman tucked hers into the waistband of her trousers, and they squatted down and began connecting the computer's entrails into a doughy mass. "Didn't intend to do it this way. But you came along. Didn't they use to call that 'serendipitous'? For us, not you. Computer'll make it easier; nobody has to hold it..."

"Oh, you learned some things here, didn't you," Mike taunted.

"And you, you fell for it, sold out to them!" He lunged at Mike. "Gotta use your mind to advance their plans. Pay for your education. Clean up messes they make. The great envireng!" He shook a fist at the sky.

"Give your sermon somewhere else. I've heard it before. *Mallacht Dé ort.*"

Catherine realized what Mike was doing; every gibe she made distracted the students, and at the particular curse she'd just spoken, they went motionless for a few seconds. But it was a dangerous gamble.

Richard also appeared to know what she was up to. He scowled at the three nervous ones who hovered near Connor and Catherine. "Shut up, you. Did they tell you, what a shame so many people had to die; we'll do better next time— So long as it's them not dying." He ranted, working in agitation, the adjustments he was making to the bomb punctuated with his words.

"Been thinking about it a while, have you," Mike said.

"Little reg babies, and letting them turn you into a petri dish; which's better, Newsman: dying knowing there's things to cure it they won't give you, or living like paralyzed spider? —No, you stay there," as Connor took a step.

The other students were fidgeting nervously at the tirade. Catherine edged closer to Connor, who had partly shielded Virginia beneath his coat.

"You got it fixed yet, man?" one asked. "We could just save this one for another time—"

"No, you stay over there," he told Catherine. "Baby stays with Newsman. Them first. Serves you right, letting them choose for you. Protecting her—" he spat in Mike's direction. "Nice pile of bodies for them to find. Prominent newsman, pitiful little child, and, then, Micaela Sánchez, brilliant graduate..." He hesitated at a sudden shift in the wind, glanced upward with a frown.

"Rear wall's coming," Mike said with a smile.

"Shut up."

In three steps Catherine would have been able to roundhouse him; he was smaller than she, she could do it— At the second step two of the three students scrambled forward and jerked her back. Bleached-hair took his charge gun from one of them and pointed it at Connor and Virginia.

"Don't do it!"

He shrugged. "Ask for permission to have another one."

Catherine's shriek was echoed by one from the woman who held the makeshift bomb as Mike kicked her weapon from her waistband. In the moment it took Bleached-hair to whirl around, Mike had rolled on the ground, snatched the gun, aimed one blast at him. His arms flew wide, his hair standing on end as the charge went through him, and he fell back on the pavement, twitching. Dropping the baby onto the ground as gently as he could, Connor hoisted one of the slack-jawed students restraining Catherine and flung him into the thorny hedge. The other one let go, backed away, ran up the twisting drive, soon lost to their sight.

"You bitch!" the woman screamed at Mike. She lifted the doughy bomb over her head, advanced upon the baby. Mike aimed once more, higher now, and turned her eyes away as an electric sizzle hit the computer. The woman screamed again, in a different pitch.

"Get behind the van!" Mike scooped Virginia up and shoved Catherine in front of her. They huddled over the child, Connor turning his back, leaping away from the student who seemed to be desperately trying and unable to remove her hands from the object she held. The explosion sent a gust of hot air and debris billowing under the vehicle. It was quick, over in a handful of seconds. The woman lay charred and smoking where she had stood. Bleached-hair, the right side of his coat burning fitfully, still twitched and made little raspy sounds in his throat.

"Stupid fools would've never got that door open with that," Mike said disdainfully. Then she looked up, took a deep breath.

"What—?" But Connor knew.

"Oh, my God."

They raced back to the shelter, ignoring the two bodies, unconcerned about where the other students had fled. Connor beat his fist against the shiny steel door and yelled, then recalled the amplifier and nudged Bleached-hair's body to one side to uncover it; but the device was black and coated with cooked flesh. He stared in revulsion.

"No time," Mike said frantically, "and it's sealed anyway." Catherine sprinted to the van.

"Not safe! Window's gone. That building!" She pointed to a temple-like edifice on a slight rise some two hundred meters off. Catherine wrapped her arms around Virginia and held her head down as the rain began in renewed fury, tinted lightly with something else in a glowing haze. They ran hard, outstripping Mike, Connor urging Catherine on and at last holding out his arms in a breathless question. She stopped to wait for Mike, who'd halted behind them and stared unseeingly.

"It's here," she said.

Catherine held out her hand and watched the drops forming rivulets, faintly orange, melting away and dripping down onto the ground in pools that shimmered with iridescence. She fell to her knees, Virginia a squirming bundle beneath her chest, and stretched out her arms into the rain like a bird protecting a chick.

Latitude N 35
Longitude W 78.4
Wind Speed 59 knots

i

IT WAS a sultry downpour, spawned by distant tropical seas two weeks earlier. It fell now tinted a glowing shade of sunset left over from those seas, and Catherine huddled on top of Virginia and waited. The baby struggled, pushed against her mother's chest to free herself from the human cave in which she was trapped. "Op!"

Catherine murmured soothing sounds and patted her head and felt the pleasant rain heating her.

"What's happening, Mike?" she heard Connor yell.

"How should I know?"

"We're all still alive. Catherine?"

She raised her head and felt rivers gushing down her forehead, making her blink and rub her eyes to clear them. Connor squatted several meters away, Mike crouching behind him. Virginia clutched Catherine's waist and hid her face in her shirt.

"Isn't it supposed to be fast?"

Mike leaped up. "Let's get to that building. Hurry!"

"Why? It hasn't killed us. If it was going to, wouldn't it have already?"

"Come on!" She held out her hand to Catherine, who finally stood with Virginia clinging like a baby monkey. "Maybe it would've, maybe not. I don't know. Thing is, no point in soaking more up."

Connor loped unhurriedly beside them. "Come on. How smart are we, standing out in the middle of a hurricane?"

They trotted on to the building which, Catherine saw as they approached, was a chapel of a kind not built for more than a century. Mike shouted through the wind as they ran: "You may already have it, but no—sense—in—" she panted, doubled over at the waist. Catherine thought she was going to be sick again and held out her hand. "No—it's all right—" Mike heaved another breath. "No sense in hanging out in it."

Catherine feared the doors were locked, but they were not and swung open when they leaned against them. The three of them stood in slowly enlarging pools that reflected oily sheens. It was a smaller building than it had seemed, the ancient wooden trims peeling and faded in spots, the marble floor worn and cracked. Perhaps it had been designed to emanate comfort and peace, its interior white pilasters bracketing empty spaces which might have held art work of some sort. Scratch marks on the marble showed where there'd been seating some time. Now it was empty of decoration and seats and eerily echoed their voices and slightest movements.

Virginia wrestled to get down. After a moment's thought—the child had not been able to stretch for an hour and a half—Catherine let her totter through the empty hall and followed after to steer her away from several windows lacking panes.

"Why worry now about a few drops getting on her," Connor said.

"This place hasn't been used in a while," Mike remarked, rubbing a finger against the edge of one of the glassless windows. "I never came here. It was like the joke of campus, haunted house at a carnival. —No, water doesn't matter now, but like I said, we don't know what's happened in us. It could've changed into something that accumulates. Like radiation. It had some of that. So we may as well stay out of it."

Virginia, unhampered by her wet clothing, grew braver. Catherine followed as she started to trot from one end of the hall-like room to the other, giggling, then turning to run another way. The other two watched silently for a moment. When the child tired and became interested in tracing the patterns in the marble with a finger, Catherine sat down at last, her back against a pilaster. "Wish I'd thought to grab the things I bought in Columbia. I could do with a drink."

"Plenty of water—" Connor tilted his head toward the window.

"It's not funny," Mike said. "You didn't see what I did at the techlab. Just let's stay out of it. It's one more thing they don't have a treatment for. One more alteration."

"You work for envireng. What's your best guess?"

"I'm not one of them.... That cretin back there. That Richard—I was assigned to design that stupid dome. I did it. I never worked in the biolabs."

"Yet I remember you talking about what happened in the experiments they ran on the Eutopix," Connor said, his voice smooth, a tight smile on his face.

"I didn't run them. I was told to watch." She stopped, fidgeted.

"But why? It shouldn't have had anything to do with that dome." Connor leaned against the wall, waiting.

"It was just part of that course, making sure you could design for the worst scenarios. The Eutopix stuff was dangerous enough. I'd never want to do that other stuff, work on the new biotes. They're always rushing the biotes. Trying to get new things."

"Why?" Connor said again. Catherine watched him uneasily, wanted to say something, to warn Mike as she tapped her foot and rattled on.

"You know, you remember how it was. People used the old things so much—penicillin, sulfas…it was the same with transportation, houses, fuel, everything. They were warned about overusing, and they'd conserve like hell, but it was always too late. They knew when it was happening, but it was like everything else: Oh, something new'll turn up."

"Blind faith," he sneered.

"And then all that stuff was sold out of Asia…all the old microbes and bacteria cold-stored, nobody even remembering how bad it was, how bad it could be. Stored, like there was something useful about it. And, you know, it *was* useful, just not…" She stopped, gave Connor a suspicious glance, walked to a window.

"How long's the thing supposed to blow?"

"You did all the investigating, right. You should know." She sat down suddenly on the floor beside Virginia and moved her hand along the marble seams like a large spider. The baby giggled.

"Got a kid sister," she explained. Connor observed in silence, ignoring Catherine's mute attempts to attract his attention.

"So why was the stuff microencapsulated, Mike? Why not, say, liquid, or something else?"

"You ask a lot of questions."

"What else are we gonna do right now? It's my job to find out about things, ask questions. So, encapsulization…?"

"It wouldn't hold up as a liquid," she muttered, her voice resounding in the chapel. "They tried. You know how they treat cancers, Connor? You must, you know everything, right?"

He rolled his eyes.

"You've done stories on it. So answer *my* question now."

"Surgery, chemicals, radiation…"

"Yeah. Poisons. Poison something to an inch of killing the patient, hope for the best. Everybody used to believe the cure was just a year or two away, ten on the outside. So here we are, still doing the same things." She went on: "Next?"

"I remember my history. The antibiotics were gone. They went to synthetics. Pretty soon they were gone too, or used so much they were useless. So they went back to poisons. Do I have that right?"

"Well, you're old, maybe you saw it firsthand, I don't know," she needled. "Yeah: They'd push the poisons into primary sites, then they learned to target them to bioreceptors, so they could be done orally or even dermally. No needles. Just apply them."

"You look tired, Mike," Catherine interrupted, suddenly annoyed at Connor's insistence.

"I'm not tired. I've only been nearly killed several times in the last hour, weather and chemicals and people, you name it—why'd I be tired?" She took a shuddering breath.

"So that's why they microencapsulated," Connor mused. "They needed it to bond with the chemical makeup of human skin."

Some of their words sounded familiar to Catherine, bringing back bits of things Victoria and David had argued about recently. She'd paid little attention to the subject of their quarrel at the time, only to the tension growing between them.

She listened now.

"Build it into the coating of the poisons, make it safer." Mike nodded. "No cross-contamination in the environment, with other mammals, plants...just rub it on, let it absorb, go straight to its receptor site."

"But Eutopix wasn't an antibiotic. It was a tranquilizer."

Virginia giggled, kicking her feet at Mike's mock spider. "But that was what they needed. Maybe it would make all the malcontents, dissidents, whatever, be less violent."

"So they gave it to them?" Catherine asked.

"Distribute it like mail at their camps, you kidding? That was what they were protesting. The ones that bought all that stuff out of Asia, airdropping a canister here, a few vials there, kill off a thousand people to make their point—" her voice rose— "they didn't care, like giving chicken pox to the Maya. And in the meantime antibiotics gone, vaccines on a shelf... And all those people die..." She stared out at the rain, and in the pause Catherine remembered more of that argument.

"You kill off fifteen percent of a population," Mike went on, somber now, "who grows the food, who does the manufacturing? Not enough to eat. No safe place to live. Quarantines. Unrest, people blowing things up."

"But the Eutopix..." In Catherine's mind strands were combining, and instead of drooping eyelids and blood she saw visions of the two of them, the classwork, the compcorder David was quoting from, the white feathery tendrils floating around Victoria's angry face....

"It worked when terrorists airdropped bacteria, viruses, poisons, right? They just had to find the correct receptor, and then they'd make a bunch of it. They'd use it for riots they expected, anytime things happened. Do you know about that stuff they called tear gas?"

Another term she recalled one of them throwing at the other, that day...but her expression told Mike she didn't know, couldn't remember exactly, and Mike went on: "It was this stuff police sprayed on crowds. Burn your eyes, your nose, make you forget whatever reason you'd been rioting; you just wanted the pain to stop. Eutopix was supposed to be humane tear gas. You were supposed to go home wondering why you were unhappy...for a few days, anyway." She laughed again, the edge in her laugh sending a thrill up Catherine's spine. "They needed it fast, too many riots, so they flash-sealed it with ozone. Ozone. Eutopix. It's funny from a certain perspective, now." The laugh became louder and more wracking. She sat down with her face on her knees. "My God, that bastard Richard nearly killed us all. Do you know that? We could've died."

Connor sat down near her. "But we didn't," he said. "Ozone?"

"Unstable. You don't know anything about chemistry, Connor? You act like you do, when you give the news. So you have your atom. Electrons and protons all around it. Maybe your molecules are mixed into water or a solution, you get an uneven number—an isotope, like that neptunium they used. With water, or maybe ozone, or who knows what else, Eutopix always wants to start breaking apart. That's what it does to your capillaries—" A cautious glance at Catherine, put her head down again.

"I'm glad you're handy with a charge gun," Connor said. "But you do talk a lot."

She glared at him with suspicious, alarmed eyes. "Well, you

ask a lot of questions."

He shrugged. "Thought it would distract us. Nothing else to do." He took his position at the open window again. Catherine saw him nod slightly once or twice as if answering mental questions he'd posed to himself.

Mike rocked back and forth, her arms wrapped around her knees. At an unexpectedly strong gust of wind that rattled one of the old windows, she jumped and crossed herself reflexively. "That was really close."

"You religious, Mike?" Connor said, amused. "You believe in God? After today?"

"Today especially." Her voice echoed from the distant corners of the chapel. "Today I hear Him laughing at us."

ii

THIRSTY. CATHERINE was thirsty. Hungry, too, but mostly thirsty.

The afternoon wore on. Hunger grew and, with it, the thirst was intense and parching. Virginia called for beek. Catherine examined every wall to see if there'd been any kind of plumbing, and, finding none, at last comforted the child into a disturbed nap in which she jerked and made odd sounds and plucked at the wet clothing. They were quiet as she slept, making only stray remarks when the lightning crashed especially near, and otherwise thinking their own thoughts in the hazy light that filtered through the windows. Catherine replayed in her mind the explosion, their flight from Site Three, their trip to Connor's parents, the encounter with the students. She tried to drive away the questions about how David and Victoria had died, whether it was painful, whether they were aware as their breathing slowed...whether they had thought of her and Virginia, whether those thoughts were melancholy or yearning, or, even, bitter.

It was too much. Nobody should have to think about things like that. She had to concentrate on Virginia.

Sometimes she glanced out one of the windows overlooking the gentle slope and remembered the bodies lying somewhere near the block building that housed the shelter they'd sought. She wondered how long they'd lie there, how long David and Victoria would lie before whatever crew the government organized came to retrieve them.

Another horrible thing to contemplate. She shut her eyes tight and squeezed the thought until it lay still.

Virginia. Think of Virginia. The other two could be alive. They could.

Yes, perhaps Victoria had not died. The image of David's red-smeared face she would put aside for a while, or she would go crazy, and there was Virginia. So put it aside. But there was no such image of Victoria, no time-frozen reminder stalking her mind to kill the delusions.

So, where would Victoria be, what refuge would she have found? How would she find her? Was she as scared as Catherine now, maybe in a sealed room with strangers?

Perhaps envireng had picked her up, injured but not dead, and had her somewhere or other.

She shook her head violently as the thoughts became unpleasant again. Later, later. When it could be borne.

Mike said the Eutopix molecule was supposed to have been a harmless little thing. Beneficial.

David had scoffed at her worrying about the control shelter. It would be the safest procedure anybody could ask for.

He'd tried to fool her.

—And yet he had not. Why had he requested Site Three, farthest away from the control booths, for her and Virginia? Why not Site One, or even Two? They could've watched from one of those, just as well.

Nobody can say I pulled strings, that was what he'd told her. *No charges of favoritism.*

She'd agreed. It would be best for her to be at Site Three, to spare him those accusations.

And Victoria.

She tried to squeeze back the image that had struggled out of its corner again. But it crept forward in her brain to confront her, a feathery-haired girl arguing with her father a month ago:

Why do you just accept all this diabhalta *stuff?*

David, pointing to the printed comments of the instructor: "Organization, expression, technical all, as usual, exemplary. However, no documentation for student's conclusions."

You got this lower mark because, when you're assigned a paper, you support your theories with facts; you know this by now. They've taught you. You don't have enough facts.

She'd searched his face with deep skepticism and, somehow, sadness. *I have sources...*

These are your opinions, and he'd smiled ruefully, wryly as if asking her, Don't you see you're not being logical? *Load your history text. Please.* He'd accepted that he couldn't break her protective coding on the machine; didn't even try. It was something Catherine thought he might even be proud of.

She'd grudgingly brought it up on the compcorder, and he scrolled through to point out sections dealing with the health catastrophe, the societal problems after the millennium, and she watched coldly as he commented on them.

Envireng, psyphi, you know why they began. He scrolled back a few pages, to gesture at a paragraph describing the think institute that eventually determined that the best solution was to eliminate uncertainty. *There were too many choices. Too much information for people to sort through, so much there wasn't any absolute, but only other possibilities. More choices. More uncertainty.*

So psyphi named itself the authority, as I wrote, she gestured at a page. *And what an appropriate name. Did they actually mean it to be the joke it is?*

Watching the two of them, Catherine knew, as he began making the mistake. Victoria's sarcasm had unnerved him. He tried sternness: *We are a democracy. Nobody had any choices taken away from them.* He faltered, scrolled up about ten sections further. *There was long discussion about it. Economically, socially, psyphi recommended which choice people should make. Which outcomes were most beneficial to everybody.*

Legislated them, she continued. *The point of my paper.*

His voice grew sharp and disapproving. *No, steered people toward them. Responsibility for others, the good of society.*

She'd stood glaring at him. He made another mistake and assumed her silence meant yielding. *Everybody still has the same choices they've always had,* he said, his face pleasant and reasonable again.

Yeah, and sanctions so you can't live with but one of them— the one they want you to make, she said, whirling away, snapping the compcorder shut, flicking that middle finger against her thumb over the waving white tresses.

It was too much: *You know, I ignored the bleached hair, that was fine, but I won't allow you to walk off like this, where are you going, who are you hanging around with these days—*

In her mind now Catherine heard his voice yelling as the girl slammed the front door behind her with a final insult: "Mallacht Dé ort!"

The orange tinge in the air had faded. The weight of the slumbering child in her arms had brought an ache to her shoulders. She changed positions, looked back outside. "Connor."

At the sound of her whisper, he jerked out of his own reverie and raised his brows.

"I think the rain's cleared."

He stretched his back like a cat and rose from the half-reclining position he'd sat in for some time. Mike watched languidly as he held a hand out the window he'd opened.

"You're right. Like a muddy water line cleaned out."

"Got anything I could use for a cup? Virginia's dehydrating."

"You don't want to give her that water yet," Mike said.

Connor gazed at her a moment, a half-smile on his lips, walked around, stood in the center of the chapel at last, hands in his pockets, and shrugged. "Sorry."

"Paper?"

Connor again smiled, this time at Catherine, extracted a small note pad from a breast pocket, twisted one sheet into a tiny cone. "Mike, you don't have children, do you." He held the cone out into the rain.

"No. I contracted for ten-year sanction."

"Sanction." He shook his head. "Maybe our dear friend Richard had a point." He brought the makeshift cup to Catherine.

"I wouldn't give it to her! Don't!" Mike insisted.

"Does the Eutopix have a particular taste or smell to it, Mike?"

"It had a kind of oily scent. Like hand-lotion, a little."

Catherine sniffed at the cup. "Nothing."

"I said it *had* one. Who knows what it is, now."

"What did the scent come from—the chemical or the coating?"

"I didn't do the research, I tell you."

"But you said you saw the data," Connor's voice was sharp, his eyes intent again.

Mike flinched. "I imagine the oily smell came from the encapsulation process. I think the drug had a more pungent—sort of a sharp, acid smell."

Again Catherine inhaled the aroma from the leaky cup. "Well, if I don't hurry, it won't matter, anyway. It's dripping down my hand."

"If I were a mother—" Mike began.

Connor and Catherine exchanged amused glances. Then, her eyes on Mike as she drank, she swallowed the contents of the little cup all at once, closed her eyes and sighed. "That was good. Now let's watch and see if I die. Fill it again, Connor." She took pity on Mike. "No mother would. That's how we knew you didn't have children."

Connor tossed the note pad to Mike. "Make a few more." He held the paper cup out the window again.

"I'm not going to—"

"Suit yourself. But make one for me and Catherine. Please. If it helps, think of how much you'd like to get rid of us."

She worked with quick, resentful motions, as if they'd told jokes she did not understand but suspected were at her expense. An oddly pleased expression on his face, Connor held out the little cone into the slow rain.

"Better give me whatever other ones you have ready, because the rain's stopping."

"Then we can leave," Catherine said.

Mike gave him one of the three she'd twisted and, after a brief hesitation, held the other two herself at a window. "Leave? Where do you think we'll go?"

"I'm going home," she said. "It would be where Victoria would go."

There was a heavy, uncomfortable silence after that, and she began the process of waking Virginia, who never woke easily from a nap and stretched and mewled and whimpered now and cried, "Beek!" Connor brought the fullest of the cups to her. She fed it to the greedily slurping child, who demanded more when she was finished. With a shrug, Connor held out the second one.

"What about you?"

"Mike's got mine. Right, Mike?" He smiled at the hiss that escaped the woman. "What about you?"

"I already had one. I haven't turned blue or anything, have I?"

He took the paper cone Mike disdainfully held out to him. He filled it and then drained it in one gulp. "We're all thirsty."

"Not to have had to pee, any of us," Mike muttered. "Which is good, with no bathroom here."

Connor considered this, gazing downward into the cup he'd just emptied, and met Catherine's eyes.

She shook her head. "She's not very wet. Not like some other time…"

"Has it—"

"Maybe. Maybe not." Mike turned away from the window and sat down on the floor. Catherine wondered if Mike had ever before allowed herself to look as young as she did now, the once controlled hair flying about in a halo of waves and tangles, all cosmetics washed from her face, the bruise inflicted by Franklin deep blue and red on her cheek. "We haven't eaten or drunk anything all day, except this damned rain now. Don't leap to conclusions. Either way."

"I've been thinking. While Virginia slept." Catherine chose careful words, but slowly, every choice being objectionable. "We left Site Three, we managed to get here, survived that…that incident over there, and got drenched. And we're alive. So something's changed. I've been wondering: when? Maybe it didn't get everybody. Maybe the change was quick—happened right after that plane crashed. Maybe people are still alive. I want to go back and find out. I'm not staying here—" she looked all around the corners of the chapel and shivered— "tonight."

"I don't want to do that, either," Connor agreed.

"You're both deluded. You know, you *know*, you both saw those images. You heard what Connor's parents said, they'd been watching all along. You know what they said they saw on the highway."

Catherine stroked Virginia's hair, lifting wispy strands that the rain had plastered down.

"You know. All of it. You got to accept it, Catherine."

She met Mike's eyes. "But I can't. Even if it's true, I have to find them, to see— So I can, so I can know what happened."

"Okay. I understand. But the thing is, it doesn't matter whether they lived through it or not. You'd never find them."

"Why do you say that?"

She shrugged and looked away from Connor's cold glare. "You'd never find them, either way. You'd just have to depend on what they'd tell you happened."

Connor threw the paper cup to the floor. It landed with a

sliding, splattery noise that echoed faintly in the room. "Don't do this to her. They kept very good records, Catherine. Painstaking records after the subsistence drought. Envireng was very careful, took responsibility for the accident, made sure everybody was informed what happened to their relatives."

"Yeah. The propaganda worked on you, anyway."

He stopped at the mocking tone in her voice. "How old are you, really, Mike? Because here you are, a certain age, and there are two people down there, dead. This time for sure because of you. I wonder if you're old enough to be held accountable for them."

"One of 'em was alive a while ago. I doubt it killed him."

"One, two, doesn't matter."

"So? So finally you've called me something accurate. So finally I, me, myself, I've really killed somebody. On purpose." She shrugged.

"I was doing some thinking, too. I think you were involved more than you said. I think you need to own it."

"Or else what?" It was the same expression she had turned on the students, but he didn't flinch.

"Or else I let authorities know about you. Regardless of your age. Mother said they were already looking for you. They want you."

She laughed loudly, wildly, throwing her tangled head back and sinking against the wall. "Oh, turn me in, Connor. You really want this story, don't you. Well, guess what. You can turn me in whenever you like, but they don't just want me. They want you, too. And her—" she pointed at Cathcrine "and that baby. And you know what, Connor?" She raised herself to crouch, half-squatting, her eyes narrow and enraged and peering through the wavy black strands. "All those poor bastards in their control shelters—they're lucky. They died right there." She looked from him to Virginia. "We didn't. So we live. For a while. They'll watch us. Something as changeable as Eutopix—it's bound to be a commodity."

"They destroyed all of it."

She laughed again. "Sure. Well, when you're ready for truth, I'll tell you what really happened to every *bocht lábái* in the subsistence drought. You want history, I remind you what they did after wars—well, you'd know anyway, right?—when they had lots of poisonous gas or biological weapons to destroy, blew up bombs. Made a production of it. And then, later, when everybody that watched got sick..."

The anger had disappeared from Connor's face.

"So, you want to turn me over to envireng? Think they'll thank you, let you walk away? Try it." She slumped again, her arms resting limply on her knees.

For a long time no one said anything. Then, "We have to go," Catherine whispered.

"The van's dead."

"Don't you have another broadcaster trick to resurrect it?" Mike taunted.

"Don't start that again!" he yelled. She did not shrink back but sat watching him wearily. "Be useful for a change. Help us figure something out."

"I don't know what to do. Envireng authority'll be here soon. They already know about those cretin students, and since every shelter has cellcomm, whoever's in the shelter may've told them you were there—real smart using your name, Connor."

"And they already knew yours, Micaela."

"So there we are."

"Shashan!" Virginia screamed, waddling near a sudden beam of light thrown upon the marble floor as the sun broke through tattered clouds. They stared at it for the miracle it was, and then Mike laughed.

"And look at us. We've been lying on the beach."

They held out their arms, surveying the color. Catherine yanked Virginia up and groaned at the faint orange tint of her curls.

"The coloring in the micropellets. It was intended to absorb along with the chemical, never did. We're marked."

"For life?"

"For several days, until that skin layer's replaced. They were easy to spot, the victims who survived."

"Then we can't be spotted. We have to be inconspicuous."

A terrible unease and dread filled the chapel with the first beams of the returning sunlight. Catherine and Connor rubbed at their skin, held out their hands, turning them over and over. Mike sat uncaringly on the floor, her head cocked to one side.

iii

THE NOISE began so softly that it was quite loud before it awoke them to other things besides the tone of their flesh. Mike whispered, "Down. Get down. Keep the baby quiet, Catherine. They're here."

Annoyed, Connor half-rose from the floor. Mike clutched his shirt. "Watch to see what they do. Just watch before you do anything." He gave her another angry look and pulled at the shirt, but she yanked him back down roughly. "Just wait, Connor. No harm in waiting."

Virginia did not want to be held down again. She bucked and went limp, whimpered and said, "No," until finally Catherine clasped her tightly to her breast and began humming a nursery song in her ear. Connor shook off Mike's hand at last and eased to one of the broken windows to crouch near it. The whining siren stopped suddenly with a little squeal.

"What?" Mike said.

"Looking at Richard and the girl."

His soft whisper, and even the humming, seemed to shout in the cavernous chapel. Catherine and Mike slid closer to him.

"Loading them onto gurneys," he mouthed. "Wait. Stopped for some reason—"

The crackle of a charge gun jerked their bodies as if they'd been hit, themselves. Connor leaned back, his eyes gazing at something unseen on the far wall.

"Richard. They used it on him."

"Why?"

Mike made a sound of derision.

Catherine hummed desperately, the keening sound wafting upward and around the cracked plaster walls. Mike closed her eyes and shivered.

"Stop," Connor ordered.

She put her lips close to the baby's ear, whispering straight into her head, "Play a game, Gin, quiet game, quiet for a little while. Shells, we're gonna be the shells—" She cupped her hands, held them to the child's ears. "Shh!" Virginia put her own fingers up on Catherine's face.

Connor sat on his heels, leaned against the wall near the window. "Talking to the people in the shelter. Telling them to stay inside. Till notified further. Wait."

The booming exterior speaker made them jump again. "We have provisions. There were others—a baby, and a broadcaster. William Connor, he said. The subversives were holding them outside."

"Oh, God," Mike breathed.

Connor peered with one eye through the window, then turned again and leaned against the wall. "Looking inside Catherine's van."

"Getting the code registration," Mike said.

"Shhh…quiet, quiet game," Catherine intoned. "Then they'll be searching, and come here," she whispered, feeling a strange relief. "No more hiding, anyway."

Mike shook her head, on her lips the sardonic, half-smile they'd got used to seeing today. "Everybody knows envirengs're the most superstitious people on earth. They talk big—'You can have religion, eat your candy,' but it's just talk. So they won't come here. They'll search other places first. They'll say nobody'd hide here, broken windows and all that. They'll leave us alone for a while."

"So what do we do?"

As Mike spoke, Connor had gazed at her almost spellbound. Now he shivered slightly, as if shrugging off an unpleasant daydream. "Wait till dark. We'll have to creep out, take back ways to leave."

"Going—?" Mike asked.

He started to answer her, turned back to the window.

Evening shadows made the hedgerow a dark, gloomy place. He told them the investigators used heat sensor goggles, looking around, had argued momentarily about where to search, then closed the back doors of the van and left, panning a spotlight from side to side, up in trees, down low under the shrubs. The van sped up at the junction of one of the main campus thoroughfares and left, and they eased out of the sanctuary.

Latitude N 35.5
Longitude W 77.5
Wind Speed 35 knots

i

THEY WALKED quietly, as fast as they could, in the dark on rain-saturated ground, obeying Mike's whispered directions as she led them down narrow paths between buildings, through tree-shaded groves, avoiding the major roads in or out. When they'd left the chapel, she'd at first lagged behind them, remarking softly that maybe it would be a good time for everybody to separate. Connor had turned to her, an exasperated expression on his face, and said nothing. She'd shrugged and glanced left and right. "Then we should go this way," she said, walking briskly, not looking back. Connor raised his eyebrows skeptically at Catherine; she shook her head, and they fell in line behind her.

They were suddenly at the campus boundary, apartments and classroom buildings ending beside a forest of tall, bedraggled pines that barred their way like policemen standing shoulder-to-shoulder. The buildings were all dark, their usual inhabitants maybe still huddled in designated shelters. "Energy authority always channels power to the shelters during drills," Mike hissed. "Everything's off but the street lighting."

They crept beside walls and edged into illuminated areas only reluctantly, so that Connor and Catherine were taken aback when, after a surreptitious look around, Mike darted to the front entrance of one of the apartments and kicked open the door, motioning for the others to follow her. Catherine stood inside the entry, her eyes adjusting to the darkness, as Mike threw open closets in the bedroom behind the sitting area. Connor seemed to be analyzing her actions as he had her words when they were in the chapel.

A dim glow emanated suddenly from the bedroom. "Emergency beacon. They used to call them 'flashlights.' Standard issue in students' apartments. No alarm system when the power's off," she explained, rifling the shelves. "Might as well take the opportunities we get. Here, Connor. This looks like you." She flung an exercise uniform at him. "Keep you warmer. No baby stuff, Catherine. But here's a blanket." She strode back into the sitting room with her arms full of clothing and other things. "What do you keep telling me, Connor? 'Make yourself useful'? Something like that? Well, make yourself *useful*. Go find whatever food we can carry, something to pack it in. I guess you'll expect privacy for your old self, so change in there while you're at it, bring your wet clothes out here. We'll have to destroy them. No point letting them know right away who was here. Go on!" she said impatiently, and with a faint salute he headed toward the kitchen.

"Come on; you can look for yourself," she said over her shoulder as she returned to the bedroom. Catherine followed her, gingerly lifting items of clothing that Mike flung at her, setting some aside to be examined. Mike stripped pillowcases from the bed and threw one to Catherine. "Put your wet things in this." She shed her clothes quickly into a neat pile, nudging them with her foot into the other pillowcase, strode naked to the closet and shifted hangers back and forth until she found a dark shirt and a pair of heavy pants. She began to dress as she talked: "We should take a few things—whatever a real thief would take to deal unreported. Give a false trail for a while. So dump a few things on the floor." She hefted a bin of socks and threw them into a heap, rummaged through them. "Here. Dry ones. Take several," she said, tossing them one after another to Catherine. "Can't do anything about our shoes." She changed her own socks, put them into the pillowcase with the other wet clothing, stood up and gave Catherine a look of impatience as she had Connor. "What's wrong with you? What're you waiting for? Permission from environ security? Get changed! Throw some stuff around!" She reached for Virginia and danced with her.

Catherine did as directed, cramming her sodden clothing in with Mike's. "Let's save the other for a sack. And look—" She laid the baby down and replaced her pants and shirt with a hooded fleecy jacket that closed down the front and tied with a drawstring at the bottom. She slipped an enormous pair of socks over Virginia's legs, then pushed her feet up into the bottom of the jacket and tied the drawstring tightly, so that it became a bunting. Mike helped her contrive from a sheet a sling to haul the baby. Virginia's hooded head poked up from above the sling under Catherine's chin; she giggled.

"This'll keep my hands freer," Catherine said, "in case..." She exchanged a glance with Mike, turned back to the other pillowcase and stuffed extra clothing and some towels inside. Mike fashioned another kind of sling for her own back and filled it with blankets and—shrugging—a few pieces of plain jewelry she found inside a box in the closet.

"Got to make them think theft, at least at first. Let's see what old Connor's up to," she said.

He'd found a portable food cooler of the kind the sophomore students used for the required environment survey course, and was considering each item he pushed inside the insulated sac. "You like crackers? Fruit spread? Tea?"

"How'd we heat tea?" Mike asked.

He held up an automatic lighter and pressed a switch. A bright flame burst from the tip.

"How'd we drink it?"

He pointed at several collapsible cups stacked ready to be put inside the cooler. He looked like a burglar, an odd glitter in his eyes, the neat suit gone and replaced with the navy exercise clothing Mike had chosen for him.

Mike laughed. "Catherine's overloaded. I got extra blankets and stuff. You have to carry the food. We need a canopy? Something to sleep under?"

"Weather forecast'll be wonderful, now the storm's done," he said. "We could just sleep in the open. Might be safer."

Catherine held her head under the water dispenser for fifteen seconds as the others watched silently and Virginia clutched her around the shoulders, her perch suddenly precarious. She insisted, "Beek!" when her mother had finished. Catherine took one of the cups and filled it for the child, who gulped it noisily and thirstily.

"Me, too," Mike said, thrusting her head in the bubbling stream. In a moment she wiped her face on her dark sleeve. "Anything to fill up with water?"

"Got several liters already."

"Hope you're strong. Hard to carry. Anybody for the bathroom?"

They met each other's eyes only briefly, the fear making them turn away.

"I'll go first," Catherine said.

They met again by the front entryway, once more unwilling to look at one another. "All right," Mike said. "We might as well leave together. But first—" She walked slowly around the living room, swiping a row of figurines from a shelf, pulling cushions from the divan, overturning a chair. "Ideally, we should break into a couple of other places…but no time."

Connor smiled, an ironic twist to his mouth, and went back to the food preparation area to open doors at random and put things down on the counter.

Catherine stroked Virginia's sweaty head. "It's so hot. We're dressed too warm."

"Can't be helped. Might need it later," Mike said. "Are we ready?"

They scrutinized each other: a dark-haired young woman in baggy shirt and pants with an enormous bundle slung diagonally across her back and a light in one hand; an older man dressed in an exercise suit, wearing a student's backpack bulging with objects; a mother with a child upon her chest and a small bag tied on her back between her shoulders. Connor pulled his sleeve up and poked at the wristcomp, sucked in a breath, gazed at the doorway.

"The wet things!" Mike remembered, scurrying to the bedroom to retrieve the pillowcase. "Connor, where're yours?"

He held out a bundle, and the wristcomp was covered by the sleeve that slid downward again. "Tablecloth. Mike. How is it you know…"

"Well? Know what?" she said irritably when he stopped.

He smiled a little. "Nothing." She made a scornful, impatient noise.

They peered past the ruined door. Nothing was moving. A soft breeze stirred the hedges around in front of the apartments, but there were no voices, no footsteps, no engine sounds. Still they tiptoed outside and slunk around behind the building to resume their trek, walking almost silently and soon grateful for the cooling wind as they began to sweat under their loads. The apartments yielded to undeveloped land—fields interspersed with patches of trees stretching back toward Columbia. They paused, contemplating the road ahead and the silent countryside.

"I want to know one thing." Mike's voice was uncertain and hesitating. "What's next if we manage to get back?"

Catherine started to say something but could not; Connor too was silent. Mike shrugged and shook her head. "Anyway, I think we should stay away from the open as much as we can."

"Little paranoid."

"You saw what they did to that subversive idiot. You saw it for yourself. How can you be anything but paranoid?"

"Maybe it was a mercy killing," Connor said, scoffed.

"Mercy killing? You know they don't do mercy killings anymore. Too unethical." She snorted, shifted her shoulders and began to walk.

ii

THE MOON, a little less than half-full, dimly lighted the fields to show them pools of iridescent water and streams rushing over their banks, which compelled them to return to the road and cross the electric strips programmed to frighten wild animals humanely, and use bridges, then hurry back into the safety of shadowy trees and undergrowth on the other side. Virginia, shrouded in the hooded shirt and sling, was damp with perspiration, wide-eyed and staring upward at the sky. Catherine began to hum quietly as they walked; the child looked into her mother's face, her eyes drooping and finally closing, only to jerk open occasionally when Catherine was forced to skid down a slope or cross the strips at the road's edge. The first time they had to retreat, Connor had stepped on the electrified edge without hesitation, oblivious to its presence, and had leaped away with a shiver.

"Forgot about that thing!"

"Just jump over it," Catherine urged, proceeding to demonstrate.

"No!" Mike yelled, but a sudden small cry from Virginia told her she'd yelled late.

"Damn!" Catherine said, soothing the baby.

Mike shrugged. "Those are always active, power failure or whatever. It projects a field upward. You couldn't jump it—it's there for other animals that have the same idea. If they have ideas." She laughed mirthlessly. "Just take the shock. It's mild, and if you're quick, it's over fast. Hurts worse to jump."

"How do you know?"

She sighed. "Did my share of it. We had to experience it during soph environsurv. Wanted us to see how the fauna felt trying to get over highways. Make us feel guilty we used vehicles and they didn't."

Connor shook his head, disturbed.

For a long time then they did not talk, but walked sometimes single-file, sometimes abreast, under the moon and brilliant stars, accompanied by Catherine's infrequent, absent-minded humming. The farther they went, the more often they came upon dark houses, empty, they discovered, after Connor crept silently up to the first one and skulked around to see if there were people inside. They had taken a circuitous path around that one, just in case, but the third time Connor rejoined them after a hasty reconnaissance, they only skirted the edges of the yards, where lawns gave way suddenly to fields. There was no one at home here, nor anywhere on the road. Catherine voiced a hopeful opinion that maybe the inhabitants were all sitting in shelters; Mike hissed scornfully, and they went on.

"How far can a person go in five or six hours?" Mike asked softly after a while.

"It's eight kilometers to Columbia. We could get there long before morning if we didn't have to rest," Connor said.

"We're too loaded down." She shook her head, sidestepping a gleaming rivulet that raced toward a stream they knew by the sound was somewhere to their right. "Can't hold up the pace. We'll have to stop and get rid of these clothes somewhere, anyway." She paused, then added off-handedly, "I wasn't ever much of a hiker."

"It's not too bad," Catherine said. "Really. It's just so hot."

Mike gave her a sideways glance.

"You need help with your load?" Connor asked.

"I'll manage. You have the food and water. That's worse."

"How'd you get a complete on your environsurv in less than top physical shape, Mike? They're kind of strict about that, I recall."

She stalked on.

"I mean, I thought they put you through things to make you get in shape while you were out in the field, or else," he persisted.

"I excelled in other ways. They made exceptions." She sped up to put several paces between herself and the others.

They walked on, detouring again to the road when they were blocked by a raging creek overflowing its banks in little whirlpools and eddies across their path. Connor cursed as he stepped over the electric barrier imbedded in the pavement.

"Damn it to hell," Mike added, her hair temporarily spiking.

Catherine patted Virginia's head as she jolted awake for a moment. She and Mike plodded on across the wide bridge and stopped, realizing that Connor hovered moodily over the strip.

"Would a few heavy blows disarm it for a couple of miles?"

"Don't. It'd be pinpointed on the grid instantly," Mike said urgently. "They'd know right away where we are."

"They don't know *who* we are."

"They'd know somebody was out here right now just being malicious at the very least. Stop for a minute, Connor." She gestured up and down the highway, northward, southward. The stars blinked overhead; frogs sang in the swampy lands to the west. "No vans. No traffic. No transports. Nobody's supposed to be out. Everybody's been told to stay in the shelters. Probably something like, 'We're busy cleaning up the mess. Keep inside till it's safe.' Something like that. So here's somebody outside. Doing something to the electromag. Which means that person's not dead. Which means that person knows it's a pretense." She took a few steps toward him. "Let it go. The shock's not that bad. Just wakes us up a little."

Catherine came to stand by her; they watched Connor kick idly at the strip before turning to join them. "You know how little raccoons crossed roads before the big highways? However the hell they pleased. When the vehicles came faster and faster, they adapted, started going at right angles, the shortest distance, lessening their chances of getting mashed. Like those moths around that English factory. The ones that hatched dirty-gray instead of white, to match the air, blend in... Grid. Every damn thing we have, alarms...everything on the grid. Set anything off, they know right away. We're not even as smart as a damn moth."

"Still feel the same about envireng looking over us, protecting us?" Mike taunted.

"When you were a kid, you ever wonder what the future would be like?" he continued, flailing his arms in great circles. "Oh, but you're still a kid, aren't you. I used to wonder what it'd be like when I was older."

"Yes," Catherine nodded.

"Everybody had a theory about it, Mike." He glanced backward at her. "Go read the literature. Some writers thought we'd be hedonists. Everything for pleasure. Live for the moment. Crowding, disease, hunger, everything solved, our lives easy—

machines, devices doing the work. A few doomsayers, they envisioned mind-control and privation and shortages and no privacy to think your own ideas, if you were risked having any. But it was always a different future, changed from what they saw around them right then."

They drew back warily as he marched past them, swinging his arms, jumping the strip again, his hair momentarily on end in the moonlight.

"You're the one talking a lot now," Mike said.

"First they budgeted for us, gave rewards for being thrifty. Figured out what occupation we should pursue. Strips to keep us on the right road. Strips to save the little animals. Sensors to keep us the right distance and just the right speed. Brakes to slow us down at the right time. Sanctions for vans, for electronic transfers. But nothing's all that different from a century ago; we have the same gadgets, just refined—computers, compcorders for the kids, phones, cameras. We still have disease and overcrowding. It just got hard to sort out who'd get what of the stuff we have left, who deserved it, who didn't. So we turned it over to envireng. All of it."

"You're talking too much," Mike said again. "Like you're high on something."

But he went on, "I'd never give it a thought, unless I wanted to get around it, go a little faster to a news event, bypass the code and accounts, when fuel was low and I was maxxed out. We knew how to get around it, find our Thomases whenever we needed 'em. When I was a kid, I didn't expect this. I always thought everything'd be solved by now, one way or the other. I never saw us still trying to figure it out. Did you?" He turned to Catherine, who kept a wary distance from him. "You afraid of me?"

"Maybe. You're acting strange."

"Yeah. Responsible journalist William Connor gives you news updates, weather forecasts. When I was a kid, everybody always thought it'd be figured out by now. Up until yesterday morning, I thought everything was figured out."

Catherine and Mike said nothing, and he went silent. They fell back into line behind him, several paces away, and trudged on.

iii

"WONDER *WHY* there's no traffic?" Catherine mused.

"Probably have some areas blocked," Connor muttered ahead

of them.

The two women exchanged glances. "Then we haven't realized how lucky we are to've got out at all," Mike said.

"We should listen for authority vehicles. If one came by, we'd need to know in time to hide."

Catherine felt suddenly as uncomfortable here in the open, dark countryside as she had in the chapel on campus. "Wonder how far we've walked."

Connor stopped, pushed his sleeve upward and fiddled with the wristcomp. "It's almost eleven. We left the apartment about seven-thirty. Walking as unevenly as we've had to, I'd say we've covered maybe three kilometers. Maybe a little more." He gazed at the numbers, pushed the sleeve over the tiny computer again.

"Wait." Catherine held his hand out. "Tell us the temperature, too. Virginia's really sweating."

He pushed her away brusquely. "Doesn't matter. We know it's hot. We know we have to walk regardless of how warm it is. Let's just go."

Mike grasped his shoulder and slung him around. "Excuse me, but now I'm asking. I don't like something you said. How hot is it?"

He stared them down, spread his arms wide at his sides belligerently. "Why don't you wear your own wristcomp instead of bothering me?"

It was one of the sacrifices she and David had made for the sake of owning the van. She didn't want to say that right now.

"Lost mine fighting Franklin, I guess," Mike told him. "But anyway, just tell us." She wrenched his arm again, tugged on the sleeve.

"Oh, no. Don't say it. The weather's been changed, too."

"Don't be stupid, Catherine. The chemical's gone, washed away, soaked into the ground or floating down rivers. Couldn't be affecting anything now. So what is it, Connor?" Mike said, pulling his arm to uncover the wristcomp. "I bet I know."

He jerked away, his hands clenching and unclenching. "Let it drop."

"You two know something I don't," Catherine said, "or maybe you just suspect something. I can't change this afternoon. You can't. Virginia's already exposed, just like us. Just tell me."

He studied the pavement. "It's not hot, Catherine. It's quite cool, the way it usually is after early autumn hurricanes. Fresh. Little under sixty degrees."

She gazed off down the black road toward Columbia, whose guidance beacons would usually be gleaming steel blue in the sky. "So we ought not to be warm. We ought to be almost cold."

The silence was enormous, so enormous that their ears strained to hear things besides country sounds, night noises, the csshhhh of the breeze in the tops of the trees over to their right. She took several steps away from the others, felt the quick rise and fall of Virginia's chest against her own, and rage overwhelmed her mind at being here, the two of them, standing in a soggy field, hiding like criminals in the dark, seeking a father and husband and daughter who were, as Mike said, dead. The other two stood a distance away.

"I wish we knew exactly how far it was," Mike finally said.

"Power grid's off in Columbia. Hard to say how far. The wristcomp has nothing to connect to."

"Let's get rid of the clothes. No helicopters. No vans. Good time to risk burning them."

"You said heat changed the chemical."

"It used to. Who cares now."

Catherine wrapped her arms around Virginia and struck off behind a house, walking into the edge of the trees beside the meadow in which they had stopped, pushing through thorny bushes and understory shrubbery. Connor and Mike followed silently. Catherine looked for thick brush and, finding a good patch, motioned for Connor to dump his clothing and theirs into a spot she hoped was hidden from the road. His suit, Mike's neat uniform, her own tailored pants—those newly-purchased ones, she recalled again, paid for with expensive personal frugalities—fell into a heap. He flapped the tablecloth in the air and stretched it neatly across the damp ground.

"Waterproof, I believe," he said.

Mike knelt, untied her bundle, spread a blanket over the cloth, helped Catherine open the knot that bound Virginia to her breast. Catherine laid the child in her makeshift bunting on the blanket. After wriggling to find a comfortable position, she drifted back to sleep.

The women turned to watch Connor, squatting on his haunches, studying the problem of making a fire. "Everything's too wet. Wet leaves. Wet branches. All wet."

Mike wandered away, the beacon allowing them occasional glimpses of her as she sought something deeper and deeper in the woods. Connor made cautious attempts at catching the sodden clothing aflame, his face glowing on and off with the light.

"Should I touch it?"

Catherine shrugged, one hand on the baby's back. "I wouldn't. Don't ask why. Superstition, maybe. You know: Just get rid of it, touching it brings it back."

He tapped the flame here and there to a sleeve, a skirt. The beacon swung erratically through the trees as Mike stumbled back, pulling a large section of dead log.

"Too wet," Connor remarked.

"On the outside. Inside it's so rotten it'll catch. Environsurv's got to be useful"—she spoke meaningfully to Connor—"somehow."

Catherine helped drag one end to the heap of clothing. Mike found a thick branch and dug into the log, opening up the punk to Connor's starter flame. She poked into the pile of fabric, draped the clothing onto the stick and, carefully not touching it, flung the pieces over the wood.

"We wondered about using our hands."

"Yeah. Silly of me, isn't it." There was no humor in her laugh.

Catherine watched, mesmerized, as the starter flame licked tentatively at the fabric. Then, seeing the jacket lifted that she had worn the day before, she remembered something she'd forgotten and jerked at Mike's arm. "Just a minute. The pager."

"Pager?" Mike said blankly.

"Victoria—" She stopped as the words refused to come out: *the only thing I may have left of her*. Shaking her head, she gingerly reached into the pocket of the jacket and retrieved the tiny positioner. "Souvenir," she said. Mike gazed skeptically at her and tossed the jacket onto the log, reached for other things.

"Wait." Connor found his shirt, motioned for her to bring the beacon near; they all gathered closer. He delicately lifted the bosom, where rain had fallen less heavily, and rubbed his forefinger and thumb against a spot not quite so sodden, a place that his business jacket had covered. Mike held the light steady.

"You say this stuff absorbs into humans."

"Yeah."

"And only humans."

"Supposed to. Who knows."

"Yeah, yeah, we remember. Let's see."

They leaned ever closer in the circle of light glaring down on his hand, their faces at last so close their noses bumped together. A few seconds passed. Then the faintly orange film on his fingers vanished.

"Amazing," he said.

Mike stared gloomily at the clothing. She cursed suddenly. "*Go n-imí an droch aimsir leat!*" It was one Catherine had never heard. She started to ask Mike what that meant, but Mike was tearing angrily at the punky log. Then she held the flame until it caught and threw sparks upward, igniting the synthetic fabric and devouring it.

iv

THEY KNEW they'd have to ration the water, not because of not having enough, but because they were so thirsty. They rolled it around in the collapsible cups as if it were wine, nibbled on thin wafers and dried fruit pieces, and reclined in a protective circle around Virginia on the blanket. Connor offered to stay awake if the women wanted to nap, but sleep seemed unnecessary now. Somewhere not too far away to the west they knew the stream was filling with runoff and probably overflowing, and that might cause them problems somehow when they sought the road again. But the night was still and pleasant, and the log burned low, and they gazed mutely upward.

In a while, Connor glanced again at the wristcomp and sat up, one hand across his knees, the other swirling a tantalizing final sip of water around in the cup. "What I didn't understand is why envireng tried to accelerate the iodide."

"You mean that neptunium isotope." Mike scoffed. "Sorry to tell you, some brainless drone knew just enough to be dangerous, found a little information on it, went with it. That's what happens when you get rid of the science. When envireng puts in people who've paid for their appointments. Not because they actually know anything. Hey," she jeered, "two weeks ago you were celebrating it."

"It's what they told me to say. I said it."

"Yeah. That you did. What'd you pay for *your* position?"

To Catherine the caustic gibes were like background chatter in a social event, as she kept her own thoughts to herself. Mike had stared unseeingly for some time at the log that still bore a gleaming shimmer of melted synthetic fabric. "The drones didn't understand the science; some people tried to make them understand but got nowhere. Psyphi sent us documents, confidential ones, said ending the drought, putting on a big show, it would make people trust them again. See, we can do this. All the other things'll work out down the road."

"What does that mean, 'other things'?" Connor interrupted. "Is that too 'confidential' for us drones to know?"

She sighed deeply and shrugged. "Whatever. They'd have given it to you to read out in a month. And you'd've just done it. It means new restrictions."

"New ones? Why?" Catherine asked, startled.

She gestured vaguely, and dragged her eyes at last away from the fire. "There's been a big slowdown, all this year."

"That's not what I—" He stopped.

"Yeah. We know." She laughed mirthlessly. "They gave you optimistic interpretations. You guys always believe them. They have you well trained. 'We give you our stats, you say them, we give you top billing.' Good dog."

"How big a slowdown?" he asked in a moment.

"Big enough so you won't be getting your fresh fruits except once a week. Don't be surprised when envireng ships you some nutrition supplements next month. Power minimized twelve hours a day this winter. At night, but that's when you're supposed to be asleep anyway," she added derisively. "Paid holidays postponed." She glanced at Catherine. "No sanction babies for five years."

"Five years? That's longer—" Catherine stopped.

"You planning on another one? Sorry. Guess you won't be doing it now, not with incentive support, anyway.... You know what? To hell with incentives." She glanced at Virginia, turned back to the glittering log. "So you miss the financial sanctions. Who cares. She gets another sister, maybe."

"It was as much for her as it was for us, waiting, I mean. There's not enough of anything to take care of too many at a time." She hesitated. "That's what they said."

"What they said. Maybe it's true. I just think sometimes people are inventive when they have to be. Look at us, here—" she tilted her head. "And old Connor's little raccoons crossing the road. *They* figured it out." She poked at the log with her stick. "But we do it the ethical way. We never say, 'No'; it's just that anything else is unbearable."

It was her version of the thing Victoria had argued with David.

"Before the drought, they wanted more babies, more workers. Then, after, they saw there wasn't enough stuff to go around." Mike scoffed. "So, 'Not so many babies!' They don't know how to engineer the problem."

"What else?" Connor said.

"What? Oh; restrictions? Fifty on your sanction fuel account."

Catherine gasped. "Fifty?"

"Guess you didn't need that van anyway; couldn't have used it much. And they're reducing the number of new research contracts. Good thing Theo's already on one, huh, Connor."

He shifted and glared at her. "You find all of this funny."

"Not really."

"So the psyphis wanted to distract from what's coming," Connor mused.

"And you just went along with the party." A scornful sniff. "All the rebellious students mock it, you know. 'Psyphi.' Psychology. Philosophy."

"Victoria said that word was a strange kind of joke."

"Well, she was right. Sounds like maybe she'd made some connections at the university, huh."

We don't know where she may be or what she might be up to with those kids... they could be roaming the countryside, hooking up with the insurgents....

"Psyphis," she went on darkly, "they keep us stoic. Stoicism's more ethical than irresponsible happiness. So your daughter knew about the joke, huh. See, Connor, I did get all those things you talked about, the literature things. Sci-fi." She said the word in a shrill whistle, raised her hands, waved them around spread open in front of them, the way Catherine's grandfather had once told her he'd done as a boy to distract a nervous horse. "They knew about it from old stories. They're very familiar with them. They used the word, figured it would bring up some memory in people. It's how they pick and choose between their religions—"

"Religions?" Connor interrupted. "They claim no religions.

You know that."

"Yeah." Her voice was again heavy with irony. "They've exposed the absurdities in all of them, haven't they. But then they do know to exploit them. Where'd they get that number for the age?"

He lay back upon the blanket, hands under his head, amusement in his face. "I'm sure you got a theory."

"I don't just have a theory; *I know*. I put in my time finding out. You ever study Holy Scripture, Connor?"

"Hardly."

"Oh, a psyphi convert, a true *believer*," she said scornfully. "Well, if you did, you'd find a passage in Psalms: 'The length of our days is—' "

"—'seventy years'," Catherine joined in softly, " 'or eighty if we have the strength.' "

Mike eyed her suspiciously. "Yeah, that one."

"Superstitious women," he mocked.

"My grandfather used to quote things like that all the time," Catherine said.

"The same grandfather who gave you that antique currency?"

"Yeah."

Connor rolled his eyes.

"Well, anyway, Newsman, they knew that was back in the dark parts of people's minds, too, like 'sci-fi,' something they'd forgotten or heard somebody say long ago—like Catherine's grandfather—so they used it. Unconscious memory. Psyphi. So how does it go? At seventy you get your regulation health care allotment? Right, Newsman?" He kept the same steady, amused gaze on her. "Nobody gets more than anybody else, unless it's unreported market, and those're prosecuted. And after eighty you're on your own. No more high-cost surgeries or treatments or therapies. Just your basic maintenance things. Right, Connor?"

"You know so much, quit asking me."

"You live, fine with them. They'll give you an apartment, food. They don't want you to die of starvation. That would be wrong. You don't live, then it was just scheme of things, normal course of life." She suddenly leaned her face over his. "That way, nobody'll accuse them of euthanasia," she whispered. He twitched uncomfortably, and she laughed. "Euthanasia would be unethical. This method's much easier to live with. Pardon the joke."

"There's always the contract," he said reasonably.

"Yeah. Always the contract..."

"Anyway, you're wrong," he said, settling back against the blanket and gazing upward into the clear, glittering sky. "You act like it's a secret you just found out. All of it was discussed, debated, reasonably—"

"Psyphi," she scoffed.

"No, mathematics. When people lived longer and longer, consuming proportionally so much more—more health care, more resources, more housing... Something had to give. Thank God for envireng. It wasn't till after the subsistence drought that the think tanks, the philosophers found courage to point out it wasn't ethical for elders not to give to society but just take."

"You're ballsy enough to apply that word to them?"

"What word?"

" 'Philosopher.' You think a real philosopher'd come up with something like that?"

"The contract gives elder citizens who choose it the opportunity to contribute instead of being parasites."

"Who 'choose'?" she demanded, incredulous. "You drone. 'Choose'? What choice, if the alternative is to die?"

"We all die."

"You've talked a good talk about other things, about giving over autonomy...why not this? Let me guess." She put a hand on his chest and leaned on him heavily. "Love your old father, don't you. Really wanted him to sign his contract, didn't you?" She pressed down more heavily.

"I did," he grunted, wriggled under her hand. "It was the right thing."

"You talked him into it, didn't you."

"More or less. I don't mind saying so. It was the most responsible thing he could do. He had some health problems."

"I'll bet you were *very* persuasive. 'More or less.' " She patted his cheek, punctuating her words with light slaps. "A good son. Your mother must be proud of you."

Catherine sat up. "Listen." She turned her head slowly from side to side. "I hear something."

"A vehicle," Connor said.

"You think anybody can see the fire?"

They glanced at the smoldering log. "We could put it out with some wet leaves," Connor said.

"God's sake, Newsman, that makes 'em smoke. Haven't you ever spent a night out of four walls before? Send up a beacon telling 'em where we are. You got on dark clothes. Sit in front of it."

"What if they have heat sensors?"

"They won't pick up this far, not the hand-held ones. And if they did, well, they'd get us, or the fire, either way. So what the hell."

He put himself between the log and the road, which lay far off to their east. The women crept through undergrowth to the edge of the thicket and watched two authority vans approach going northward, one on each side of the divided highway, their white paint shining eerily in the moonlight, searchlights sweeping slowly back and forth across fields next to the pavement. One of the two, the one on their side of the road, stopped in front of the tidy dark house they had passed and, as the other van idled in the opposite lane, inflicted the searchlight upon it from roofline to ground level; the windows bled white as the light assaulted them, and then went black again. A silent technician stepped out and aimed a tulip microphone at the house, donned a headset and listened for a moment. Then he stored the equipment back inside his vehicle, and both vans moved on. And there was silence once more. Mike and Catherine returned to where they had spread the blanket, hearing Connor talk softly as they drew nearer: Virginia had awakened, thirsty.

"I gave her a cup of water; I guess it was all right," he said.

Catherine stroked the child's sweaty head. "Let her have some more, if she wants it."

They sat in a circle around the baby as she gulped down a second cup and struggled in the improvised bunting to crawl to Catherine's lap. She picked her up and held her against her chest, and the child stared into the dark forest.

"So has anybody given any thought to what we're going to do?" Mike paused. "It'll be easier for you two. They might still have doubts you lived. They won't necessarily be looking for you. Theo said my name and face are everywhere. I won't have a place to hide."

"Why're you so certain we'll have to hide? If we turn up, what could they do? We could stay low until we reached the broadcast station, then just walk in—"

"And do what? Say, 'We're here, give us a party'? You're so stupid sometimes, Connor." She turned to Catherine and arranged the sling to be fastened back around Virginia. "We need to be on the way. While they're going the opposite direction from us. Everybody rested enough?"

"How old are you, Mike, really?" he asked suddenly.

"You talk too much." She jerked the blanket up from the ground and began rolling it in with towels they had used as pillows. "Why don't you gather up what we ate with, pack it again. Be useful, Connor. For some reason I don't get, Catherine has to go home, and it suits me fine to do it in the dark, and so let's get moving."

She wrestled angrily with her bundle, twisting and pummeling it before strapping it to her back. Catherine leaned against a tree, Virginia squirming against her chest, perspiring again, complaining in a soft whine. Catherine loosened the knot that bound the sling tight and unfastened the hooded shirt, working it slowly and gently over the baby's head, pulling it at last free and out. She tossed it upon the glimmering log. Connor poked at the embers until the fabric caught in a bright flame.

The baby's skin cooled immediately, and her wriggling slowed. Mike completed her frustrated mishandling of the blankets and stood, shining the beacon on the ground.

"It's unreasonable to expect you to go on with me," Catherine told her. "If you want to leave now, I'm sure Connor agrees—" she frowned at his sudden surprised exclamation— "you should do that. Authority won't be waiting to put us on trial—or whatever they intend," she finished.

"So, 'Get lost, Mike', that's it? Why not, 'Let's all go somewhere else and hide and just blend in'?"

"I have to go back." Catherine wrapped her arms around Virginia, her face lit by the beacon Mike swung upward. "I'm alive, and I have to find out about David and Victoria. I have to, Mike. I've listened to the two of you talk and argue about things I, I just don't care about. You probably don't understand. Going back's not even a choice to me."

"A reg," she mocked.

"Yeah, a reg. *I* have to find out about David and Victoria. *You* have to keep away from authority. We'll have to figure out how to get through, or around, Columbia first, and that'll be dangerous for you. So maybe you should find a way to slip off as soon as you can."

"Columbia'll be dangerous for all of us. Why won't you believe that?" she cried. "This thing, these chemicals—it was supposed to kill on contact. Or at least it did last time, in the drought. So something happened to it, or somebody did something to it, more likely, and here we are, colored up for all to see, hot as hell, drinking rivers of water, not needing sleep— Oh, what the hell. You and Connor want to walk straight into a town swarming with envirengs, why not. I guess it'd be the last thing they'd expect of us. I don't what I'd do by myself anyway. Probably walk off into that river over there."

She took three steps toward the highway before Connor grasped her arm to stop her.

"What is it we don't know?"

She gazed downward despondently as if accounting to a headmaster—sullen yet resigned, Catherine thought, the way Victoria had been when confronted with the unbreakable passcode in her compcorder. "Why're you asking? You know how it was. I already told you. Diseases. Not enough food. Employment down. Those people—" she shivered— "forced to move out of their stackhouses. They made those camps, and they grouped together in one big mass out there on the coast. Protests against the contract, envireng, sanction accounts—all of them asking, *Why're we letting these people make these decisions for us?*

"Envireng was scared of those people. But they had the Eutopix. Other stuff before'd just been experiments on old people. It was the first huge batch of anything. Just airdropped it on them while they slept." She shuddered again and turned away. "Except they woke up with their vessels bursting and died."

"But everybody knows this."

"That's what I said! You know it. They were always honest." She scoffed. "Painfully honest. Those people died—the old ones, the weak ones. The others didn't, right then. So authority moved in, mopped up, mass-cremated most of the dead ones; kept a few bodies for scientific study in labs."

"The ones that didn't die—?"

"Oh, they all died, eventually, Catherine. They all died. They could've died more comfortably. But it killed all of them.

Eventually. The ones that lived a while...they watched them. Tried to figure out how it'd happened. It was like that old disease they called 'hemophilia.' Anything made those vessels bleed. Touch them, they'd bleed.

"And then they stored the damned stuff. They'd made so much—so proud of it! Maybe it could be modified for research, pain relief—if they could figure out to keep it from killing you first." A scornful laugh. "Maybe it could be used as a weapon.... But then the insurgents started leaving for Canada, so authority decided it ought to be destroyed. They didn't want to. It had potential."

"They did destroy it," he said.

She scoffed. "Okay, sure. Some went missing several times, but it's still around, lots of it, because some fool got hold of it very recently, didn't he."

"My God."

She laughed, loudly enough that Catherine wanted to clap a hand over her mouth. "*Your* God, Connor? You haven't got a God. Kind of late to claim One now."

"So they'd take me...they'd take Virginia, if they got her, and—"

"Watch her. Yeah. Test her. Keep her in a lab somewhere— wouldn't look like one, but might as well be a lab; she'd never be anything more than an experiment from now on. Nothing to gain in destroying *her*; they have the dead ones on ice already. They'd probably let you stay with her, till you were gone. But you'll never find your husband or your daughter, Catherine. They'll tell you they had to be mass-cremated, like all the others, to be safe. Like in the drought. Sooner or later they'll tell your relatives you died, too. But you won't be as lucky as your David or your girl."

"I don't believe all that," Connor said.

"The honorable newsman. Why believe *me*?" She shrugged. "Suit yourself. You'll find *out*, yourself..."

"You're risking your freedom." She held Virginia tightly. "Just go. But I have to see, with my own eyes. I can get home on my own."

"How do you know any of this, Mike?" Connor asked, still holding her arm, shaking it. "I've been in news for—for a long time, and I never heard of it."

"Yeah. Truthful, trustworthy William Connor. But lazy, as it turns out, just mouthing what they tell you."

"You only designed that dome. Why didn't they just send you the specs, let you do your job? Why make you observe lab work?"

She jerked free and began walking away fast, pushing at the undergrowth, stumbling against trees. "I wish to God they *had* just sent the specs."

Connor rushed ahead in a bound and barred her way. She tripped and fell to the damp ground.

"Stop! Both of you!"

Mike sat up, brushed off dirt and leaves. Catherine went on: "Connor. They wanted her to know. They wanted her invested. They thought knowing what could happen would make her get it perfect." She understood now what David had told her, why she herself had been all but ordered to attend the big event, why they'd asked, *encouraged* her, to bring Virginia along as well. Not just for the optics—healthy woman, healthy baby. She knew now. "Help her up."

Connor held out his hand. "You're really clumsy."

"And Franklin was so anxious and fidgety. They can't control storms, but they can put you on a front line to make you accountable." She went on, as realization came: "They knew somebody'd got a lot of that chemical. But they weren't going to back out on doing their event, even knowing it might be sabotaged."

"You asked how old I am, Connor? I'm twenty. They tested me out of the barrio, brought my whole family here." Mike rattled on, ignoring their startled expressions. "It's what they do. I went to the best schools, upper-quadrant. They pay, if you study what they've tested you into. Maybe what they intended with your girl, with Victoria—" she turned to Catherine. "But all the intelligent ones are rebellious. They know how to handle that, though. Give 'em a max account. The more awards I got, the harder I worked, the more comfortable my family got. I failed environsurv. 'But you can still graduate; just work for us,' " she mocked. "You aren't even considered for the secret societies unless you protest against envireng. All the students do it sometime. Some don't quit. Some do, and go along with envireng.

"It was just fun at first...then it got serious, and they're always after the ones who don't go along. So they tell you, 'We'll take away all your courses, but you're so brilliant, you can finish early with our help.' Then you can't ever go back. And you can't go to what you *were*...you're Eliza Doolittle. See, Connor, I do know things about some old literature. So I went along. I specialized in biodomes after environsurv. Protect endangered habitats. Ironic, right," she added bitterly.

"So that's why those kids on campus knew you," Connor said, "why you knew how to break into apartments, how to use the charge gun. Is the group that organized?"

"Why? You want to report 'em? It's always been that organized. One day they'll get rid of envireng. I wish I'd stayed with them. We'd all be better off."

"Let's go," Catherine interrupted. She stepped carefully over the sodden ground and started singing again, quietly, as she walked ahead of the other two.

"They have us study all the philosophies, all the theologies, and then we break them into pieces in our first year. 'Surely you don't believe that...' Once they get your soul, they put it to work for them. They have you do environsurv, study the subsistence drought. Prepare yourself for the age. Nobody can consume forever; it's not responsible."

"It's not," Connor put in.

"You're disgusting. How old are *you*?" she asked, her voice strident behind Catherine, who walked ahead of them now, fast. "You got it out of me. So, how old, Connor?" she insisted, poking his side at every word with the emergency beacon.

Catherine heard irritation and something else in his voice when he finally answered: "Fifty-seven. That satisfy you?"

She laughed. "In a few years, you'll have to decide. And where'll the rebels be then, Connor? Not standing up for you, you can bet. Were you happy your poor old father got hooked up to God knows what, while they tried out new biotes on him? For the good of society, of course," she added.

"Well, he was alive. That's something."

"Yeah. It's something. He got hooked up, signed on, couldn't even decide when he gets tired of it. They'll decide for him." She trotted away from him to catch up to Catherine.

"Why don't you be quiet for a while, Mike?"

"He provoked me." She limped along beside Catherine, trying to match the brisk pace she had set. "You're walking fast."

"You don't have to stay with me. The two of you can keep

arguing and go off on your own. I'm not your referee." She said it without thinking, stopped, reconsidered the harsh words. "Did you hurt yourself when you fell?"

"Not much. One more bruise." Mike shrugged, and Catherine, remembering, glanced at her face. The moon shone overhead now, and Mike's face was shadowed from above, her neck and eyes dark, her cheeks and nose illuminated. Catherine turned her gaze away quickly and looked ahead, her pulse racing, and picked up on the song. Mike, some distance now from Connor, listened for a while to catch the tune and began humming it. Connor followed silently.

"What's that song? You been doing it all day."

"An old one. 'Scarborough Fair.' Many centuries old."

"Sing it," she demanded.

"You sound like Virginia." She didn't want to be near Mike right then, walked a few paces away, and, hearing the limping steps behind her, relented. Mike hummed an accompaniment.

> Are you going to Scarborough Fair?
>
> Parsley, sage, rosemary and thyme...
>
> Remember me to one who lives there.
>
> She once was a true love of mine.
>
> Tell her to make me a cambric shirt...
>
> Without no seams nor needlework...
>
> Tell her to wash it in yonder dry well,
>
> Where no spring flows nor rain ever fell...
>
> Tell her to hang it on yonder thorn,
>
> Which ne'er bore bloom since Adam was born...
>
> Tell her to buy me an acre of land
>
> Between the salt water and the sea sand...
>
> Tell her to plow it with one ram's horn,
>
> And sow it all o'er with one peppercorn...
>
> Tell her to reap it with a sickle of leather,
>
> And bind it all in a sheaf of heather.
>
> Then she'll be a true love of mine.

"So frustrating," Connor said loudly. "Sew an impossible shirt, buy mythical land, what's the point? We've done all that stuff today—thorns, and water, and rain, and clothes. That song is pointless. Stop. I don't like it. Do something else." Catherine heard his steps approaching on the pavement. "It's depressing," he muttered and passed the two of them.

Catherine walked on silently, and Mike kept humming.

v

THEY SAW the metal sign from a distance, its letters unlit without the urging of vans on its sensors telling it to shine its message, and drew near at a faster pace, their memories reminding them of what it said, their brains insisting it could not be so. Mike flashed the emergency beacon on the sign and stopped still. "Columbia—half a kilometer! Not possible." She gestured at the sign as Connor strode up behind them. "It can't be. We can't have got here already."

Catherine seized his sleeve and punched at the wristcomp, then looked back at the sign.

"Let's don't quarrel about it. Maybe we went faster than we thought—" he walked on.

Catherine clasped Virginia tightly to her. "We're hot. We're thirsty. We can't sleep. We walk very fast, even with these burdens."

Mike stared at the sign, glanced sideways at Virginia. "I wish I could've kept her out of it, Catherine." she whispered. I've got little sisters. I wouldn't've deliberately..."

"What made you two not to take my van yesterday?" Catherine asked, her eyes level on the younger woman's, who stared back a moment before answering.

"We decided it wouldn't be ethical," she said bluntly at last. Connor added nothing.

Latitude N 36
Longitude W 76.1
Wind Speed 29 knots

IN A way, 35 wasn't surprised when the door swung open with a buzz, no other warning. He knew they'd eventually show up. Still, in the dead of night, no power but only an emergency light, he experienced a quick thrill up his back, his eyes widened, a momentary idea about leaping out his window crossed his mind, before he turned calmly to face the three of them.

"Hello," he said. "So glad you don't stand on ceremony."

—That ancient, disused expression, yet everybody knew envireng found such things delightful. And the sarcasm seemed to make them happy. They all smiled as if invited into a celebration. One gestured to the other two, who separated off in search for whatever, opening doors to his bedroom, his bath.

It would take them a while to find the hidden lab. But they would, finally; probably not today, though. He was glad he'd moved the extra mice to 19's apartment. 19 would feed them.

"Am I allowed to bring some personal things?"

The face of the one standing there crinkled into a broader smile; they loved it when you used courtesies under duress. The question…it conceded you had to ask them for basics, and that acknowledged their power; but if you did it with politeness, that proved you understood the hollowness of the ethics behind the question.

Because they could always just disallow anything and everything.

But not this envireng: "Certainly. And by all means bring your notebooks and documents."

"Notebooks? Documents?" He affected confusion, this time eliciting a tiny sound that could've been the start of a chuckle. Game engaged.

"We're aware you didn't allow it on the net. Very, very clever choice. So you must have hand-produced documents, and it would be wonderful for you to bring them along. And, definitely, clothing if you like. Personal toiletries."

One of the others returned empty-handed. "Nothing."

"Favorite food. Whatever, to make your new life more comfortable," the first one continued.

The third returned with a satchel bulging with folders. So, that one had picked up everything from the top of the desk.

The first one touched, patted the satchel and turned a hopeful, expectant gaze on 35, and so he continued the gambit and produced a sucked-in breath, a slightly shocked expression…don't overdo it, he reminded himself. That took away the fun.

The envireng beamed with pleasure. The others hovered near the door, uncertainty on their faces, as they didn't comprehend; but this one and 35 nodded once, almost imperceptibly, at each other: respect.

"We're interested in your research. You'll have plenty of time now to elucidate it for us, if you *choose*."

Envireng was civilized. No death penalties, no tear gas, no unpleasant hand restraints—all unnecessary, since they'd figured out how to harness the electricity into their charge guns. 35 held up an index finger, for permission, found a backpack in a cabinet and put in several things—sleepwear, comb, shaver, and so on—and walked genially out his door with the other three.

He and they, 35 and the envireng, they'd have merry days dancing that tarantella. But those *diabhalta bastards* would never decode his notes, which weren't there, anyway, not in that satchel, and they'd never find out that when he recorded "neptunium" he meant "progeria gene mutation"—he was proud, justifiably proud, of having discovered how the original chemical sparked that deviance—and "Eutopix", that was really "Ebola." He'd learned if the Ebola didn't survive the process and kill you, the other would. He'd felt sorry for the mice; he couldn't always identify which component was the culprit.

"*Mallacht Dé ort*," he swore softly in the parking area, one final touch that caused reflexive twitches in the other envirengs, but brought a mischievous twinkle to the first one's eyes; obviously, to him it was unexpected, but appreciated, frosting on that cake. But it was enough; don't overdo it. So, only to himself, in his mind, he added, "*Nár chuire Dia ar do leas thú.*"

Latitude N 36
Longitude W 76.1
Wind Speed 29 knots

THE SILENT, deserted habitations nearer the campus had lulled them into dangerous carelessness. They approached Columbia in near silence, individual thoughts holding them in a kind of forced solitude, close as they physically were. Open countryside yielded to orderly, planned residential areas again. They stopped near the official town border and drank deeply from the last liter of water in Connor's backpack, saving the final bit for Virginia, when she awakened. Then they gazed unseeingly at the neatly landscaped but wind-blown streets ahead of them.

As they passed in front of one row of dark apartments, the sudden barking of a dog made them jump. They realized then they'd seen no pets on the road, owners maybe having taken them along to the shelters. They froze, laughed a little nervously, and froze again at the unexpected sound of a voice from one of the apartments.

"Quiet, Suzie! Anybody out there?"

As one, they darted silently into the black shadow of the apartments, the moon deep in the west, and edged along the wall until they had put the dog and its owner far behind them.

They had walked over eight kilometers with the comfortable, foolish notion that they wouldn't see other beings.

They were more careful after that, and disturbed, also, to realize they didn't want to be found out, wanted to avoid human contact, even benign human contact.

"We burned the clothes assuming nobody'd catch up to us for a while," Catherine said, interrupting the silence. "What if they do, today?"

Connor shook his head. "Can't think like that."

"But we have to," she insisted. "What if some of us are caught, but some of us get away—"

"Only if we split up," Mike said pointedly.

Catherine paused. "Well, but what if it happened, anyway? Whichever of us was left—who'd we try to contact? You, Will. Who'd you want to find out what happened to you?"

He nodded to indicate something ahead of them. "If they're still alive."

"Nobody else? Family, children?"

He turned a sardonic gaze on her. "No kids. My wife wanted them…. I bought in like you. We divorced long ago."

"Because of that?"

"Who knows? Maybe. Partly. Liked the financial benefits of abiding by sanction. Like you."

She started to object and remembered their family planning according to guidelines, the basic but new van allowed them as a reward for their frugality; it sat now dead and probably still on campus where they'd left it. She turned to Mike, who leaned against a great oak tree, some of its branches torn or stripped of leaves.

"I don't have anybody to tell," she said without looking at the other two. "If they get me, they'll make a big production of it anyway. Have a hearing, convict me of crimes against humanity, then turn ethical and sentence me to live the rest of my life away from that humanity. But I wouldn't. I'd be in a lab." She focused on something the others did not see far away, and sighed. "So it doesn't matter. If I get away, I know how to get in touch with my family. Don't worry about telling anybody about me."

"What about you, Catherine?" Connor said after a moment.

"If you can keep Virginia somehow, get in touch with my parents." She laughed wryly and Connor lifted his brows. "They're in Canada."

Mike shifted her position against the tree and smiled.

"They left right before Victoria was born. My grandfather wouldn't sign his end-will decision. He was one of the first group. They didn't know what to do with those people. They had to sign something, some way. Authority had to have some decision from them. He wouldn't. They threatened to put him in custody for a while, and he left. Actually, I think they let him go, maybe even encouraged it. My grandmother'd already died; my parents agreed with him, and they took an excursion tour of Minnesota and just crossed the border and met up with him."

"You know where they are?"

"They move around. Sometimes British Columbia. Sometimes Manitoba. I can give you a network gridsite, but, Connor…" She took a step nearer him, looked up into his face. "You can't betray them with it."

"Canada doesn't have an extradite agreement anymore; they repealed it after the drought," he said. " 'Crazy Americans', you know, 'totalitarian government,' all that."

"Yeah, but, Connor..." She edged closer, her face barely six inches from his. "They know envireng would like to find them, yank them back. Make them say they were selfish. Use it for publicity."

"Like the dome," Connor said.

"If they were determined enough to go to Canada, what makes you think they'd give in to envireng?" Mike asked.

"You did," Catherine told her. "If they can get the most rebellious student minds, I don't think it'd be too hard for them to manipulate older people who've become more...philosophical—"

"Cynical," Connor interrupted.

"—about everything anyway."

"Why didn't you go with them?" he asked.

She closed her eyes, remembering from twenty-five years back. "David and I thought people had done such a lousy job of managing things. Disease out of control, resources stretched thin. We had more confidence in authority."

"And you were too risky for them to have along with them, unless you agreed with their point of view," Connor said.

She laughed mirthlessly. "That, too. In other words."

"So your children—"

"They've never seen them."

"I'd think they wouldn't approve of your going along with sanction reg before Virginia was born."

She walked away silently.

"Your grandfather still alive?"

"He died eight years ago. I know, because my parents and I keep in touch. In ways."

"So the money you gave Thomas probably had sentimental value. Besides being antique." When she did not answer this remark either, he went on. "I'll see about getting it back from Thomas."

"If he survived."

"I'm betting he did."

Virginia was stirring and stretching in her usual way of waking herself. Catherine leaned against the tree and spoke briskly:

"Connor, you haven't said so, but I'm holding you to be trustworthy. In David's and my sanction account listings, there's an inventory line detailing Virginia's toys. One entry lists an imported item—I'd rather not say it out loud. Sometimes lately I wonder if envireng hasn't even got microphones hidden in the street lights."

" 'Big Brother is watching you'," he mocked.

"Yeah," she agreed, aware of Mike's confused expression. "The grim vision."

"Resources are too scarce for them to eavesdrop on everybody. At least we have that much to be glad for."

Mike ambled away from them. "One thing's for sure. We've changed since yesterday morning. Band of revolutionaries here, aren't we. Slandering envireng, whispering conspiracies."

"We didn't change," Connor said grimly. "We were like this before, only didn't say it, not even to ourselves. Not admitting it. The address, Catherine."

She told him the code that hid the gridsite, watched him close his eyes and memorize it.

"Wonder if there're other people like us. Thinking but not saying it."

Mike rolled her eyes. "Why'd you think they sweep the campuses so much?"

"What do we do now? It's almost daylight."

He glanced around at the quiet, dark houses and apartments and walked on to an intersection as Mike and Catherine followed. They huddled together at the street's edge, feeling naked and exposed as he considered the two roads. "We could go this way and avoid most of the major streets. Take longer, though."

"Hey, we're speedwalkers now," Mike said.

"Something in me wants to be careful," he went on. "Nothing stirring…but all the same… We ought to find a safe spot before light. We should go to Mother and Father's."

"Oh, I see," Mike said. "She can't look for her people, but you can for yours. Hypocrite."

"No. No. Just, if they didn't live, or if they're not there, we can rest in their apartment, maybe…"

Mike scoffed.

"How'll I get back home? It's too far to walk that part."

He looked at her with a troubled frown on his face. "You still want to do that, Catherine? I sort of agree with Mike. Not sure about this…"

"About damn time."

"Going back won't be easy, or maybe a good idea, either."

"I rescued you both in my own van," Catherine said. "You wouldn't have got out if I hadn't. You don't want to go all the way back with me, fine, I'll do it myself. But you're helping me find a way. You owe me that. Then you want to stay here in Columbia, or go somewhere else, that's your business. You don't have to keep going with me to my home."

"Fair enough."

They walked single-file again, the women following the path he took down deserted avenues, slipping between shrubbery and walls, hugging brick and siding so closely that it caught on their clothing and hair occasionally. There was no more conversation, only apprehension and resentment and mistrust. Catherine clasped Virginia tightly against her chest at one muddy stretch and, looking down, discovered the baby was fully awake, regarding her with a serious, knowing countenance that roused anger in her again. How dared they. She couldn't decide whom to direct the anger at— Connor, who seemed happy to go his own way here, once he had his goal accomplished; or Mike, who'd been so difficult and still was, so hard on her nerves the whole time; or someone else. The insurgent in the plane. Envireng itself.

They approached the stackhouses obliquely, creeping through empty lots, keeping near thicker vegetation whenever it was available. Connor had slowed down, reluctant, it seemed, to cross the last half-block to the back of the apartment complex, though the building cast a dark umbra which hid them from the early morning glow in the sky. Catherine felt another brief moment of sympathy for him, and steeled her resolve by recalling his plan to abandon her here yesterday and, perhaps, even now.

They hesitated along the back wall.

"What're we waiting for?" Mike whispered, fidgeting. "It's getting light, Connor, dammit, let's go in."

"No sign of anybody," he mused. His breath seemed abnormally loud and fast. As if he was recovering from a morning run.

"They're in shelters, stupid, it's where they were told to be. Or in the basement or something. Look, I'm going on. You two can stand out here if you like, wait for authority to pick you up, but not me." She trotted along beside the wall until suddenly her feet slipped on the treacherous wet earth and she landed on knees and hands on the ground. Connor again helped her up.

"I'm understanding why you failed environsurv. You're going to look like we've been beating you." He took a step back in shock.

"What?" she asked.

Catherine shook her head at him.

"What?" Mike demanded.

"You're muddy. You look like a street urchin. Let's go. Come on, Micaela." He drawled the name, turned it into a sentence, making each vowel a separate word in length, changing her alarmed expression into a scowl. She frowned blackly at him, rubbed her hands and the knees of her pants.

He tried the manual override on the door at the rear of the stackhouses. "Security's on. Must be some power here—" and pressed his finger into the ID panel. Access was granted finally, after some moments longer than he thought should have been necessary, and they crept inside the black central entrance where the only light came through narrow windows at the east-facing front of the building. They stood blinking in the dim hall. "Which way to your parents'?" Mike asked.

"Down the loggia, to the left," he said.

She turned away from him and strode ahead, oblivious to the disturbed glance Connor shared with Catherine, who shook her head again.

"I noticed it back on the highway. Just let her find out on her own."

"You know she's lying. There's something big she hasn't told."

"She's said a lot, Connor."

"Yeah. But she knows more." He grimaced and edged cautiously onward.

Preoccupied with their own anxieties—Connor glancing at the narrow windows, two of them broken by branches thrown in the storm—they caught up with Mike as she counted doors and marched onward. "This ought to be it, isn't it, Connor, Newsman, this's it, right?"

He shoved her away and drew an uneven breath as he pressed

his finger into the ID panel.

Access granted.

Catherine pushed him aside. "Let me. You wait here."

She began unwrapping the sling as she made her way cautiously through the dark sitting room. The sheet she dropped on the floor somewhere, and she shifted Virginia to her hip and tried to peer through the eerie shadows to see what she could, strained to listen for sounds she hoped to hear. A low, monotonous buzz led her to the back room; a strange draft of cool breeze that cleansed the house of its antiseptic smell confused her. Remembering the screen images at Site One, she turned Virginia's face into her shoulder to shield her from whatever she might see and stepped into the room.

The breeze had come through a window they'd opened behind the chair, a weakened hum from the discarded feeder box still lying on the floor. The buzz masked the old man's light snores. They were asleep, both of them, curled together in the big contract-care reclining chair, Connor's mother half-leaning against the old man's shoulder. Catherine smiled and walked back into the front sitting room.

"They're all right. Sleeping."

Connor rubbed his arms and shivered violently as one would do who left a freezing night to enter a warm house, then brushed past her to go to the back room. She followed in a run. "Don't wake them up; it's not six yet—"

But he had already lighted the room as she spoke, and she followed him to see the old people arising from the chair comfortably, unhurriedly, as if they frequently awoke to find people standing over them. Connor uttered a curse and closed the window with a bang.

The old man cackled loudly, fumbling with buttons on the side of the chair to lift it to an upright position. Ruth smoothed her hair. "So you did get—" She stopped and, giving each of them a head-to-toe, assessing look. Joined in the laugh.

"What wardrobe choices. I thought you were always professional, Will."

The old man struggled to his feet, holding onto the arm and then the back of the chair as he raised the window again. He leaned outward, breathed deeply with his eyes closed. "I do like a fresh breeze."

"May I please clean up?" Mike said, holding out her muddy hands.

"Come with me, child."

"Look." She flailed her hands out briefly. "You have to call me something. Just say 'Mike.'"

" 'Mike'?"

"You've heard, you know it's really 'Micaela.' But everybody…well, anyway. I go by 'Mike.' So, just… It's strange for you to call me 'child' all the time. I'm hardly a child."

"Yes, she is," Connor said blandly; she hissed at him as she followed Ruth from the room. Connor stood away from his father, watching the old man breathe in the cool air at the open window, before turning suddenly, another half-smothered curse on his lips, to brighten the lighting in the room. He reached out and lifted up the old man's chin.

"What'd you do—dance around in it?"

"Oh, no—too many branches flying here and there. Just opened the window."

"What's that, Will?" Ruth asked, returning.

"What'd he do—go out and tap dance?"

"No. We just decided to open the window—" She gestured to demonstrate, and Connor sucked in a heavy breath.

"You, too!"

"Well, on the other hand, Will, I know you haven't been to Jamaica lately."

He rubbed the back of his left hand disconcertedly and then stuffed both hands in his pockets. In the silence, they heard running water as Mike washed, and a loud exclamation—"Holy Mother of God!"—and the tap was turned off.

"She saw it," Catherine remarked.

In the pantry-kitchen Ruth began opening cabinet doors to pull out boxes. "Why don't we sit down and have breakfast."

"Religious girl," Connor said.

"How'd you get here, Son?" the old man asked. "They blocked the main highways long ago."

"Walked."

"Walked? All of you? With that baby? I'm impressed."

"Why're you even up? Shouldn't you be sitting down?"

"Hell, no!" The old man's voice rose, and he grabbed the chair to steady himself. "Sat down too long. Feel stronger standing. So why'd you walk?"

"Her van was...disabled on campus, kids playing guerrilla. You just opened the window, held out your hands—?"

The old man beamed and leaned on the edge of the chair. Rubbing her face, Mike wandered back into the sitting room, her arms clean, her thin form clad in one of Ruth's house robes.

"Rinsed my pants, hung them in your bathroom. You know what I think? We ought to scrape all this stuff we can out of the drains and roadsides and bottle it. No bruise. I had a bruise on my face when we were in that apartment." She glanced at the Connors. "When we were at this one place. In the mirror, I saw a bruise, and do you see one now?"

"It was gone a while ago," Catherine told her. "Ruth, is it all right to let Virginia down? She's been in a sling for a long time."

They found resting places, Connor on the floor near the open window at which he gazed from time to time, Mike slightly apart from the others and between them and the hallway to the bathroom, Catherine leaning against a sofa. Ruth passed around a tin of brightly-colored cookies and, a moment later, mugs of hot tea, which brought a wry smile to Catherine's face. "Tea. We got tea."

"Told you we needed tea. Don't need it hot, though," Connor added.

"Pretty warm these days, seems like." The old man winked at them.

The baby wandered around, toddling back and forth from Catherine to Mike, who played with her and cajoled her into eating and drinking. With a touch Ruth turned down the lamps that were presently unnecessary, as the sunrise flooded through the front room and hallway into the back. Each time the wind gently pushed aside the curtain at the window, Connor turned his gaze there and frowned.

They talked little, listening to Mike and Virginia's game, enjoying the counterfeit moment of peace. Virginia's diaper needed replacing, a problem accomplished when Ruth brought out a carton of absorbent pads which Theo scoffed at. Ruth took scissors and a linen towel and fashioned a tunic for the child with a few metal fasteners. Catherine waited for the friendly routine to stop as the day wore on and the light grew. They glanced surreptitiously at each other's arms, rubbing the flesh, and busied themselves folding the things stolen from the campus apartment, cleaning up the breakfast crumbs. Tension grew almost palpably. Mike inched backwards until her spine touched the wall, then slumped and stared moodily at her spread fingers on her knees. They all jerked when the screen came to life in the middle of a news program. Ruth approached it and faced them all, silent but questioning.

Connor shook his head. "Not yet."

She touched a button, and the screen was black again.

"What're *your* plans, Son?" The old man snickered.

Connor didn't join Theo's laugh. He closed his eyes, avoided Catherine's glance. "I don't know."

"Your mother and I watched, after the rain stopped, until they reduced power. They want to know what might've happened to you. And to Mike."

"Have they mentioned anything about David, or me and Virginia, or Victoria?"

He shook his head. "Nothing. But they'd like to see Will. And this young lady. Do *you* have any idea where you're headed?"

Mike flexed her fingers.

"Catherine says she has to go home, try to find out where her husband is, her daughter."

"Reasonable."

"No, it's not reasonable!" Mike said, rousing suddenly from her lethargic pose. "They have them somewhere on ice. They'll tell her it's too bad, they have to be cremated or something, and then they'll see where she's been..." She pushed up the sleeves of the robe and displayed her arms. "And that's the last we'll hear of her, too. No. It's not reasonable." She seemed to shrink backward again into a smaller shape than before as they looked at her.

"How do you know, Mike?"

"I know."

"She knows, Mother," Connor agreed. "But Catherine feels she must go back."

"And you'll go with her," Theo said firmly. "She stayed with both of you when she didn't have to."

"Ethical," Mike scoffed.

Remembering her resolve earlier in the morning, Catherine found herself standing, as if something cold, something hardening fast, had been poured into her. "I can do this alone. I already said I would. I knew the two of you would never go with me. You have what you wanted, Connor. You're done. But I need a vehicle."

Theo pointed at Connor, who abruptly raked his fingers through his hair several times, lifting it in spikes that reminded Catherine of yesterday, of him standing on the platform at Site Three.

"Use ours," Ruth said.

"Your fuel allowance is not enough to do her any good,"

"Don't think I heard that, not from you, Will. When did you ever let that slow you down?"

"But there's something in what Mike says," Ruth went on. "What will you do after you get there, Catherine? How will you find out anything? And then where will you go?"

Connor hadn't said he would go with her; she really would have to do it herself, just she and Virginia. The cold iron continued to take shape in her body. "They'll have lists by now. I'll go back to the house—"

"And do what?" Mike objected shrilly again. "They've probably sealed your house. That noise—" she nodded at the feeder box— "it's nothing compared to what the sealing tape makes when it's broken."

"How do you know?" Connor asked.

"They use it in the techlab every time an experiment goes wrong. Keep fools from blundering in before it's cleansed."

"I see."

A great silence filled the room, so much so that their ears hissed like the empty seashells. They stared at other things, unwilling to make a decision for her, and at last Catherine took a deep, heavy breath. "We all got through it alive, even you here in Columbia. Somewhere between here and home something happened to that stuff and it didn't kill everybody, and that means there might be some hope. And even if there's not any," she went on more loudly, as Mike cursed and shook her head, "I still have to know. I still have to, Mike. I don't expect you to understand. And you and Connor can just stay here and be safe." She was pleased to see Connor flinch at the bitter word.

"You'd be safer with her, I'm thinking," Theo remarked.

"Let's look at this logically." Connor straightened from his slump, gazing out the window. "I told those people in the ranking shelter who I was."

"Stupid," Mike commented.

"On the other hand, they already knew you," he pointed out with a sudden fierce glance at her, "so authority's aware we were there, on campus. And if you're right, they know Catherine was there, too, because of her van, and they know about the baby."

"Too much information to those people in that shelter," Mike moaned.

"We didn't have a choice, you remember?" he retorted. Observing his parent's puzzled frowns, he jerked his hands through his hair again. "What happened is—"

"Later. Go on."

"So. So. We didn't get into the shelter. They've probably checked the other ones by now, know we weren't there either. And if the power grid's up on campus, too, that apartment's screaming, and they may have got around to looking at it." He rubbed his hands up and down across his stubble. "Mike says survivors will be a commodity. I think I believe her. I saw them kill one of the students. He'd tried to kill us, so I had no sympathy for him. But he was alive...and then they killed him for no reason I could see."

"He'd been out in the rain," Mike said sardonically. "He was pretty far gone because of...well, an explosion...hurt. But not quite dead. Still fresh."

Ruth gazed at her with revulsion. A grim smile crept across Theo's mouth.

"So assume Mike's not psychotic or paranoid. You go back in Mother's van, Catherine—I'll take care of the fuel, but you go back, you ask—who do you ask, Catherine? Where do you go?" He paced in front of her, meeting her eyes as she stared back at him. "Looking the way we look, all of us—" he jerked at his sleeves— "looking this way, how can any of us go anywhere for a while? I would help you, Catherine—"

"No, you wouldn't," she said bitterly.

He stopped in front of her, hands on his head. "But I swear I don't know how. To help. I don't know. I can't see anything for you to do. After you go to your home, find out whatever—where then? You just want to start driving."

"She's got relatives in Canada," Mike reminded him. Theo laughed loudly.

"Drive to Canada by herself?"

"Right now I'm going home."

"That's insane."

Mike approached Connor to argue and poke at his chest, and Virginia demanded to be picked up. In her mother's arms she watched the clamor with an interested smile on her face…too interested, Catherine decided. She edged around Ruth, who was tapping Theo's shoulder, trying to calm him, and took the baby into the front room, away from the buzz and stubborn voices and guffaws. Virginia wanted down, and ambled about, touching the few pieces of bricabrac Ruth had placed here and there to give the stackhouse comfort. Catherine eased down upon the divan in the room and dropped her head upon her hands as the child wandered around.

Presently the crackle and electronic voice of the ID panel roused her from empty dullness she'd found refuge in. She stared uncomprehending as a series of numbers was read off in the static, dead tones—no name, no vocal identification, only numbers keyed slowly one by one, as if to guard against mistakes. A long string of numbers.

She realized the Connors and Mike had stopped yelling at each other. Connor came around the edge of the passageway and glared at the panel that continued calling out its numbers. Mike followed him, reached to nudge his back again and stopped, her mouth open, her breath coming fast and panting as she listened to the spoken digits. "Envireng."

"They can't do this," Connor began. "This isn't possible, even for—"

"The override sequence. I know it." She turned and stumbled away, looking for an exit, a place to hide.

Access granted.

The front door swung open, the glaring sunlight framing the man from behind with an unearthly halo that shone around him and cast his face into black relief.

Latitude N 37.1
Longitude W 75.7
Wind Speed 30 knots

i

CONNOR KICKED the feeder box against the wall. When the dying hum persisted, he wrestled the screen from the window and threw the black rectangle into the back lot behind the apartments and turned to the man standing in the doorway.

"Destruction of authority equipment," the man commented pleasantly. "Was there a problem with the chemfeeder, Mrs. Connor?"

In the pause then, as the five people considered an answer to this question, the man glanced around, assessing them. Mike shrank back against the wall, her chin dropped low upon her chest. The door behind the man slowly closed.

"It came loose," Ruth began softly. "In the storm. A frightening thing. It came loose—the wind was so strong, breaking the front windows—"

The man smiled amiably. "We could have repaired it. We had other things to deal with." Another gaze around at them. "We came as soon as we could, when the alarm was registered."

"Holy Mother of God," Mike whispered.

His gaze turned back to her.

"Every damned thing's wired in to you people," Connor raged. "I had access to documents. Always—they always said privacy's inviolable. Privacy's always guaranteed."

The man continued to smile. "Mr. William Connor, yes?"

"Why're you here?"

"As I said, we're responding to the malfunction in your father's chemfeed line. As we always do. When an occasional malfunction happens, obviously any interruption in the continuum is a blow to the whole study. And, also, of course—" he smiled— "potentially dangerous to the patient." Glancing again at Catherine and Mike, he extracted a tiny transmitter comp from his pocket and pressed buttons. The oval relay dish on Ruth's table came to life with a beep, pinpoints of light racing across the pearly surface in a few seconds. He returned the transcomp to the pocket and smiled once more. "So then. Let's see what we'll do to restore the chemline."

Theo pointed a finger like a beacon; the man took a few steps toward him and halted suddenly. Their eyes steady on each other, they hesitated.

"Mr. Connor," the man said sternly. "You signed the contract." There was something condescending in the man's voice, something Catherine found insulting to an older person.

"I do hereby cancel it," Theo countered.

"You can't."

"He can," Connor burst in. "I didn't think you could override somebody's personal entry. Seems many things can be done."

"How're you planning to hook me back up?" Theo went on. "You going to do it by yourself?"

"I won't need help, will I. You'll be responsible about it."

"I may not."

Another sequence of numbers interrupted them—a shorter one, punched rapidly into the ID panel. Coldly furious, Connor observed the door open and a tall, thin man in technician navy enter carrying a black leather case.

"So you even changed his code," Connor said.

Silent, the technician began removing items from the case, laying them on a small round table near the hallway. The last item was a charge gun, which he casually hefted once and held as he paused in his preparations, bestowing on each one of the adults in turn a contemptuous glance.

"There're four of us," Connor remarked.

"Five!" Theo disagreed, standing up straighter, one thin hand clutching the soft covering on the chair. "You can't keep us here."

The envireng's expression remained unchanged, pleasant, bland, even. "None of you will be going anywhere just yet."

Connor glanced at Mike, who only stared back at him. "I've learned some things. Been told some things. I have a theory: I think this chemical speeds up cell activity."

"Which chemical are you theorizing about, Mr. Connor?" the envireng asked.

"You've looked at us since you came in. You know what we've been exposed to. I think the chemical sped everything up."

"You have some kind of reasoning to advance this theory of yours."

Catherine pulled Virginia into her arms, drawing the

momentary attention of the armed technician.

"I do. We're all thirsty. We walk faster, need less sleep. We seem to heal—" Connor faltered and turned back to Theo, a frozen something Catherine thought looked like terror and sudden comprehension on his face.

"You've figured it out," the envireng said with deep sarcasm. He picked through the items on the table and lifted some. "You can put the others back. We won't be using them now," he told the technician, who started replacing things into the black case with his left hand even as he kept cool watch over them and held the charge gun in his right hand.

"You figured it out," the envireng repeated, connecting tubes and bolts with swift motions. "Very recently, very recently, within a few hours, we learned of some interesting research— Well, your father'll be contributing data, you all will. A new direction, beneficial to all citizens. Now, Mr. Theo Connor, we're going to attach this chemline."

Theo again pointed at him as if delivering a judgment. "Flee from the coming wrath!"

The envireng paused for a second, a twitch, then a scoff. Mike giggled.

Connor continued, "There're five of us. Two of you."

"Not for long." The technician smiled.

Connor considered this and remembered the sparkling pinpoints earlier on the oval relay.

"Mr. William Connor, you've seen the improvement in your father's condition."

"You could start all the experiments you want to in the regular way—" Catherine interjected.

"We could, but we've been spared the time and expense and trouble of conducting preliminary work," he went on, "we've been given a broad human study. A tragedy, in some respects, and we sympathize with those who, like you—" he paused— "didn't actually choose. But this is an opportunity. And consider your contributions, Miss Sánchez, Ms. Millen." He shook his head in disbelief at their involuntary gasps. "You don't think we wouldn't know by now who you are, where you've been? Although we didn't really hope you'd come here," he mused. "We thought you'd be more cautious."

"I'm sorry, Catherine," Connor said.

"How broad an experiment?" she asked, wondering about David and Victoria.

"There're five of us," Connor said.

"How repetitive. A disappointment. Expected more from such a respected journalist." His eyes seemed genuinely sad.

"You've requisitioned backup," Catherine remarked. "And additional transport."

"Take any personal items you'd like, you can easily carry. It's not terrible, you know. Everything you need's provided. And now, Mr. Theo, we need to reconnect you."

"I think accelerated cell metabolism would confer greater strength," Catherine said, advancing slowly on the technician and passing the baby to Ruth.

"Not necessarily. But one thing it does *not* confer is immortality," the envireng said sharply. "I assure you. We know that...regrettably. Some stupid, rash choices—"

In an unexpected blur of actions she couldn't sort out clearly later, Catherine saw Theo throw something, and there was a sudden struggle, and the envireng was on the floor, moaning, the contents of a broken tube splashed across his face, and there were curses and the electric sizzle she recognized and more bodies tumbling to the floor.

"Time to go," Ruth said calmly.

ii

SHE WAS even more efficient than they themselves had been in the campus apartment. With the baby still in her arms, she gathered up absorbent pads and several extra items that could be converted into clothing for Virginia, then gave instructions to the two women who stood as if bolted to the floor, staring at the bodies. "Mike, dear, you have to transmit whatever's necessary to hold off the backups. Can you do that?"

Mike turned uncomprehending eyes to her.

"Do you know codes that would be accepted?" Ruth urged.

Mike opened her mouth, but when no words came out, she merely nodded.

"There's always some kind of routine thing they do...to say things are satisfactory, I believe. It'll need to be done...perhaps you could say something about a dangerous spill, an accident?"

"Yes. An accident." Mike shook her head in short, agitated arcs right and left, darted to the transmitter and began carefully punching in numbers.

"Catherine, their transport will have to be disabled. I really don't know anything about that. Can you manage?"

"I've seen it done," she said. "Tell Mike she should indicate a pump failure. Tubes disconnected, stuff leaking." She paused at the front entrance, turned back. "Are you...?"

"I'm all right."

Catherine almost asked another question, thought it would be better to wait, took a quick glance out the front, sped outside when she observed no movement.

By the time she returned carrying a handful of wires which she dropped into a bin in the pantry, Ruth had tied up many things into bundles and stacked others neatly in boxes, having commanded obedience from Mike, who stood behind her awaiting more orders. The robe flapped around her arms as she swung them in nervous agitation.

"You two are clever," Ruth said. "I believe everything's arranged as well as we can manage."

"Tech backup's been called off, Mike?" Catherine asked.

"For a while. I can't promise much."

"Well, whoever does get here'll have to depend on whatever transport they bring. I yanked anything I could find in the general location those kids on campus did."

"We should go," Ruth urged quietly. "We can carry all these things at once without having to come back up here."

"You take Virginia. I'll get these—" Catherine swung two of the soft bundles onto her back and held them with one hand. "And this carton."

"It's too much for you."

"I'll just balance it on my hip. And Mike knows about charge guns. She should have it."

Ruth set Virginia down and knelt beside Theo, straightening his arms and legs which had lain at strange angles that made him look like a disjointed puppet. She spread an afghan over him and patted his face. Catherine and Mike juggled their burdens into positions as comfortable as they could contrive and waited for a signal.

"I'm ready. We should go."

Ruth took the child back into her arms and walked without

hesitating toward the front of the stackhouse, Mike following her as she'd followed Catherine the day before. Catherine slowed, turned back, sighed. She eased the box from her hip to the small table, shoving the envireng's miscellany off, and laid the soft, heavy bundles down beside her. She squatted beside Connor and massaged the top of his shoulders.

"It has to wait. Remember telling me yesterday? It has to wait."

He raised his eyes but stayed slumped over, arms laid upon his Indian-crossed legs as he sat beside Theo. Catherine again patted his shoulders, urging him upward, but he stared motionlessly at the gently swaying curtain. Her eyes sought the object his were focused on, and she understood.

"They did it on purpose. Connor, he expected it yesterday. He was ready then. They opened it on purpose."

"I ruined everything. I shouldn't have brought you all back here. We should've walked on to your home."

"We couldn't have, you know. It was too far. And they'd've just taken him wherever Mike says they'd take all of us. You spared him that."

He rose from the floor finally and turned to gaze at the paralyzed envireng, whose wide, darting eyes, the only indication of life in him except a faint twitch of his chest, frantically returned the stare.

"I hope you die," Connor said. "I imagine you intended Father to get what you got. Something to keep him paralyzed but alive. A specimen. Maybe you got a little too much?"

With the toe of his muddy shoe he nudged the man's shoulder. "I did a report once on curare. An ancient bush poison. This's something like curare, isn't it? Did you watch my report? You think maybe it works on your mind last, so you're aware of things being done to you you have no control over?"

"Stop," Catherine said.

"Maybe we can perform some experiments on you. Right here, right now. Fire, maybe? A knife?" He found one in the tech's bag, brandished it.

The terrified eyes stared upward. The chest jerked slightly.

"Enough, Connor. Let it go."

He prodded the envireng one more time. "A chonách san ort. I know a few myself," he told Cathcrine. He stepped over the body of the tech, whose uniform smoked a little in a small circle on his torso, evidence of what a charge gun pressed tight against a body would do. "Here, give it to me," he said brusquely as she hefted the box again. "I could at least be useful. Where's Mike? She should be telling me that."

Ruth and Mike had stopped at the front entrance, where Mike stood cautiously pressing one digit after another into the entry panel. "They locked us in. After Catherine went outside, they locked us in somehow. I need another... another, um..." She stared intently at the scrolling information and bit her lower lip. They waited silently, patiently, aware of their dependence on her ability to override this new obstacle. Virginia leaned around on Ruth's shoulder. "Beek?"

"She says she wants something to drink," Catherine explained.

The panel at last granted them permission to exit as Ruth was giving the child a long guzzle of juice from the cooler. Ruth glanced around the room, then momentarily at the hallway behind which the three bodies lay. Connor shifted from one foot to another.

"Is there anything you want me to get, Ruth?" Mike said softly. "A memento—anything—?"

"This wasn't really our home. It was a research lab." She glanced back at the hallway and absent-mindedly stroked Virginia's hair. Catherine mutely urged Connor to speak to his mother, but he did not, looking down into the box he held, running the fingers of his right hand around the top edges of it.

"Then let's go," Mike said, and led them out, charge gun held at an angle away from her.

They almost expected to see white envireng vehicles lined up in the lot, but there were none. They slung the soft bundles into Ruth's old van and slid the boxes beneath seats. Ruth fretted about not having restraints for Virginia, while Connor worked underneath the raised hood of the vehicle. In a moment he had joined them inside, pausing to consider which way to go.

"I won't ask any of you to do what I have to, to find out what I have to," Catherine told them. "Not now. Just take me back there and leave, get on out. We don't know how much time Mike bought us—"

"Not much."

"They'll be watching for us after they go inside there—" she nodded toward the stackhouses.

"I made you go everywhere I wanted to—here, campus, back here again...It's your turn," Connor said quietly.

"You can't go back!"

"You feel so strongly about it, Mike, get out and do whatever you have to."

He eased the old van from the lot. They glanced at the white envireng vehicle as they passed it, its hood up as if an open mouth calling for help. "I hope you messed it up, Catherine."

"I did my best."

Mike took a deep, shivery breath. "Look. You've added two more bodies. You think after this—after it being an envireng, and a tech, too, Connor—you think they won't pull out everything to look for us? And the positioning chip—"

"They're not supposed to use that." He paused.

"Yeah, well, they're not supposed to do lots of things, but they do. Why else would it be there? They'll have us located right away."

"Rip it out," Catherine said.

"Can't. You didn't own your van very long, did you? You take the chip out, it disables the engine. Everything's worse now than it was before that man showed up. Why'd you kill that tech, Connor? Couldn't you've just disarmed him, restrained him somehow?"

"No matter who goes with me, we need a strategy," Catherine said. "I suggest the back roads again, if Connor's willing to do the driving. After I find out whatever I can about Victoria and David, then..." She stared for a moment out the window. "After that, we'll probably have to leave, fast. Where?"

"Mike said you had relatives in Canada."

"Canada's a long way from here. The envireng back there—" she tossed her head—"knew who we were, said nobody thought we'd show up."

"I'm sorry," Connor mumbled.

"Which means they've probably been trying to monitor us, figure us out, may have accessed and frozen our accounts. All of us. We use them, they'll know. How'll we arrange fuel?"

No one offered answers.

"Everybody agree about the road, at least?" Connor had brought the van to a halt at the intersection of the small, quiet lane into the larger highway. They felt conspicuous, the only vehicle in sight. Catherine saw curtains move gently in windows of a few houses to her right, as if the occupants were as frightened of them as they were of being seen. "Drive on. Don't dawdle here."

"Anybody who wants out, this's a good spot to leave," he persisted. "Anybody—?"

"Shut up!" Mike screamed, flailing her arms.

"Not one more word from you about bailing out. You understand?"

Her lips closed tightly together, and he turned to the left. South.

"Get off this highway at the very first old exit," Ruth said.

"Right."

They remained silent, muscles straining, urging the van on. When they had travelled a few kilometers, Connor swore bitterly and turned left, taking them off the broad road into tree-lined lanes. No one asked why.

The residential area behind them, they arrived at the junction of modern street and old highway, the sharp curve to the right prodding them back to the electromag road, another lump of sodden earth, bleeding down its sides, denoting the failure of a financially-doomed public improvement. The old roads were supposed to have been destroyed in huge sections, not heaped with mounds of earth, Catherine knew. But after the drought, envireng had lacked funds to do it, so the ancient byways were ignored, the theory being that they would finally be covered with vines and debris and, at last, thick vegetation like long-lost civilizations from millennia ago.

Roman roads, the Appian Way. Mayan temples. Ancient, dying cultures. David had said that. They'd used precious fuel sanction to roam around one day soon after getting their poolvan. The sudden freedom had left them giddy.

Connor steered around the dirt mound.

Catherine roused from her mournful reverie. "Do you suppose your old friend Thomas could help with fuel?"

"Can't take the station with us," Connor muttered.

"But maybe, dealing unreported...maybe he knows of other places that would. All along the way. Afterwards."

Connor kept close watch on the debris-strewn road and shrugged.

"He's barely functional, Catherine," Mike said. "He hardly knows how to operate that modern equipment he has."

"When did you meet Thomas?"

"On the way out yesterday. We had to leave the electromag—so many people on it, so crowded, nobody able to go fast enough to get away from the...the storm... Connor took us to Thomas's fuel station, because the fuel was used up fast when we subverted the strips..." She saw Mike's involuntary shiver and felt her own body convulse suddenly. She rubbed her arms, looked down at the tone on her skin, glanced at Virginia's glowing face. "Anyway, Ruth, he seemed to be the sort who'd help—"

"He would if he could," Connor interrupted. "If he can."

"How'd you pay him?" Ruth asked, a smile lifting the edge of her mouth.

"Catherine had money. Real money," Mike said. "Here, right here with you: somebody that keeps currency. Not for a collection. For purchasing things."

"And you were glad to see it," Connor reminder her grimly.

Ruth gave Virginia another long drink from a bottle she'd packed into one of the boxes. "None of you would be here if not for something you did, or had, or thought of. Catherine's vehicle brought you away from the observation site. It must have been very hard for her to leave, after what happened there. Then she purchased fuel to bring you to Columbia, to the university. Will knew the roads, knew who to buy the fuel from."

"Don't forget how handy he is with codes," Mike said, rolling her eyes.

"Yes, he always was that. A good thing right now. And then, you, Mike, you knew about authority protocol."

"And anarchy," Connor remarked. "Burglary."

"You've brayed about obeying authority, and people having to be made to do right...but how'd you know Thomas? You've put in *your* time defying authority, haven't you. It's worse being sanctimonious than it is just outright defiant. Just stop." Mike clutched the seat as he swerved suddenly to avoid a limb at the edge of the decayed highway. "Who was it said, 'Thank God for envireng'? 'Thank God for envireng.' A convert."

"I'm no convert."

"A convert now against envireng, anyway."

"Anarchist's words. From a weapons expert," he mocked.

"I didn't kill the last one," she said. "You did that one yourself."

He turned furious eyes to hers for a brief moment before

concentrating again on the road. "I'm not burdened by that body in Columbia."

"Which one?" she taunted. "There were three." She waited for another response, and when none came, she went on: "Who bought into all the stuff about the age, and the contract? Who bragged about making his father sign?"

He raked fingers through his wild, oddly-tinted hair. Ruth had been listening in consternation and reached out a hand, drawing it back just as quickly.

"God, Mother. I never told him—it was because I didn't want him to die. I just didn't want him to die. He never knew why I made him sign it."

"Oh, he knew. And he knew you'd figure it out, sometime."

Catherine closed her eyes and leaned her face against the window.

iii

THEY WERE better prepared this time. The river would have to be crossed somewhere, and, not hearing the roar and hiss of a hurricane at their backs, they had time to seek out other twisting paths until they found a bridge that had not been dismantled. The van was quiet, Ruth only talking to Virginia, playing counting games.

Thomas was using a blower to move piles of leaves and twigs from the pavement when Connor stopped. "Old fool," Mike whispered in amusement. "Ignoring what they said about staying in. Out here for the world to see."

The blower was loud; Thomas, his back to them, didn't hear their arrival but, turning to herd a pile of stray leaves into the main heap, looked up with a start at the sight of the old van. For a moment he stood motionless, confounded by their presence. Then he laid the blower down and advanced.

"What you doing back here, Willie?" He craned his wrinkled, scrawny neck around in the window and saw Catherine and Ruth and the baby. "So, I bet you came to collect your old money."

Catherine smiled.

"Where's Theo?" he asked Ruth.

It was the first time Catherine had seen Ruth's face anything other than smooth and expressionless. She leaned back, the smile frozen, and blinked. Connor examined the steering wheel, ignoring the question. Thomas's eyes flicked from the son to the mother.

"Well, I hope to hell he took one or two with him," he remarked.

"He did." Catherine leaned forward past Ruth. "Thomas, do you have a place we could get out of the open here…can you let us into the service cubicle or something? Can you help us go off the grid? We really don't need to be seen just yet."

He shuffled away and with sudden, vigorous energy, opened the doors they'd driven through the day before when the sky was ashen-gray and the rain drenching. This afternoon, with the sun just beginning the second half of its circuit overhead, it seemed odd to be inside the cubicle. Connor instructed the vehicle to shut itself off and exited to stand by the old man as the heavy door slid shut on soft, pneumatic hinges. Mike watched daylight reducing itself in an ever-diminishing bar and turned around to look out the front of the van at the tall shelves of ancient cans bedecked with cobwebs. She smiled again.

Catherine removed Virginia from the back seat. "I didn't come for my money, Thomas." She paused as the old man, his face registering horror, suddenly gripped her arm and then Connor's.

"Good God Almighty."

"Don't say such awful things around him," Mike said, leaping out.

"Good God Almighty. Are you out of your minds? Coming back here, looking like that?"

"Yes," Mike said.

"I have to try to find out what happened to my husband. And my daughter. I'm responsible for their being here—" she nodded toward Connor.

"No. We came willingly," Ruth said.

"You're crazy to be here. How'd you manage to get past road blocks? Out of Columbia?"

"Road blocks?" Mike twitched.

"I listen. I get the broadcasts. I stayed in my shelter till the rain quit. Officials said to stay put till they gave an all clear. Any goat with sense knows that'd mean till they got things arranged to suit them. I listen. They had road blocks, Willie. They cordoned off everything south of Columbia this noon. Just a while ago."

"So it was still deadly—"

"All the way from the site to, oh, five kilometers from here.

Nobody spared, they said. Then, for some reason—"

"Electricity?" Mike interrupted. "Did they say 'ozone'?"

He glanced at her. "Everybody north of that seemed to live."

"How'd you know?" she went on. "That wouldn't be public information yet. They'd want to round up everybody they could that got exposed, try to convince anybody else they weren't given a dose of the original stuff."

Ruth was listening again with revulsion.

"It was what they did, before," she finished simply. They all stared at her. "So how do you know where the line was drawn? Envireng'd never let that out just yet."

The old man met her cool gaze with suspicion. "And you wouldn't know that without being one of 'em."

She held out her hands, Ruth's robe still flopping and floating around the thin arms. Thomas flinched.

"At least tell us if you know it for a fact."

"I know it for fact," he said.

"Catherine?"

They stood in a semicircle in front of her. She laid her face in the rosy strands of Virginia's hair and closed her eyes, at last weeping quietly until the child began to squirm and pat her face questioningly. She heard whispers. When she lifted her head again, they had all moved away a distance and stood in silence, watching her. Thomas motioned vaguely; Connor shrugged as if answering a difficult question that had no answer.

"You want to see the casualty lists?"

iv

MIKE WHISPERED a string of curses as they followed the old man through a door he unlocked using a complicated sequence of codes. Catherine would've laughed at the words, except that she felt she was traversing one of the dark rounds of Hades, some place where every insignificant sound—even the curses—echoed with sinister undertones. They entered a narrow, dirty hallway illuminated—when Thomas touched a switch—only by a dim, antique incandescent bulb suspended from some point out of their vision. A tattered religious poster was tacked to the wall opposite the door; a large crucifix gleamed beside it. Catherine, standing near Connor, felt his sudden shiver. Mike whistled in appreciation. His nearly-bald head shining underneath the dangling bulb, the old man beamed at their reactions.

"They don't go any further than this when they've done inspections. This stops 'em. Always curious why I have that lock on that door. ***What you hiding, old man?*** I act ashamed, let 'em come in here. They stop quick, back out again. Every time." He laughed; the echo made Connor shiver.

"Thomas, Theo would have loved it."

"Yeah." He turned suddenly, awkwardly. "Well. They never see *this*." He reached down to the floor, patted the concrete until he found something which turned into a dull gray handle, and, giving a mighty tug, lifted another flat, square door upward to open a black hole in front of them. Mike scampered over and peered into the abyss.

"What the hell do you have down there?"

He was delighted at her interest and fumbled under the edge of the hole. The ancient bulb over them went out suddenly. They were in complete darkness for a moment. Catherine was aware of Connor's quick breaths beside her; Virginia twisted around in fear until another light came on underneath them. Teetering over the edge, Mike grinned, her face bleached by the gleam of modern illumination. The old man squatted beside the trap door, like a spider, Catherine thought, and beamed as the robe-clad girl clambered down steeply-inclined steps. "Next..."

Catherine followed, the baby clutching her around her neck, and Connor helped his mother down. Thomas came last, gently easing the door back into place and sliding an enormous, flat bolt to lock it from the inside.

Mike pivoted from one flat screen to another, to the small oval relay, to the keypad beside a set of headphones. The tunnel was cramped and narrow, more a reinforced trench in the ground than an outpost. Catherine gently touched the white wall on one side; and, as if understanding her curiosity, Thomas patted the other side.

"Here's my shelter. Had to excavate right next to it so the snoops wouldn't find a large room I couldn't explain." With a look of prideful satisfaction, he waved at a small white cube in the far corner. "Have a drink of something." He glanced around as they laughed.

"What can you do in here?" Connor tentatively stroked the keypad.

The old man sprang into one of the two chairs. "I promised this lady a look at the casualty lists. That's first."

"You can't access their casualty lists," Mike argued, leaning over his shoulder as he clicked long sequences. "They wouldn't—" She stopped and cursed again, as the screen filled with names.

Connor shoved the other chair at his mother. Catherine dropped Virginia on Ruth's lap as she sat down: "Get her something to drink—" and, pushing Mike aside, knelt in front of the display. Alphabetized names scrolled off monotonously for two frames, when, to Catherine's irritation, Connor paged backward to the first.

"What're you doing?"

"This looks like thousands. Thousands. Let me see how many per page—"

She grasped his hand tightly. "It can wait."

"Fifty-seven," Mike said. "Now you count the frames, Connor, if that's what you're interested in. Go on, Catherine."

The list scrolled down. Now and then she saw the name of one of Victoria's classmates she knew, and as the M's began, she breathed harder. Mike adjusted the speed to a slow crawl, leaning over, her finger hovering above the pause button. And there it was: David Millen.

"Stop."

Mike pressed the pause key. Catherine stared at the name, displayed in cobalt blue upon gray, an electronic tombstone in the underground catacomb.

"Your daughter's not on it," Connor said after a moment.

Mike turned around to the old man. "Is there a separate 'Missing' list?"

Connor reengaged the scroller and scanned the remaining M's, then increased the speed. "Let's try the end. Maybe if they have one, it's there."

He finished as Catherine stared blankly. The list ended abruptly. No additional categories. He returned to the section on which David's name appeared. Mike tapped her fingers on the top of the oval relay. Once more they waited for Catherine. The screen blinked suddenly, causing them all to jump.

"They update it once in a while," Thomas remarked.

Catherine gazed at David's name, the screen a glowing impersonal memorial. She dropped her face to the counter. "This is worse than before. I don't know what to do now."

Mike cast an impatient, annoyed glance at her. "There's not anything much else *to* do."

"Shut up. You see any of her classmates' names?" Connor asked.

"Several. I didn't know them all. She had other friends. Second-quadrant. Third-, even. None of them are there. But they weren't invited...they weren't invited to observe."

Connor leaned closer to the screen; Mike was running a finger down the columns. "Maybe they miscoded her name."

"It's not here." Mike shook her head. "No 'Victorias' at all."

"I may never know, then." The enormity of it pressed upon her, dragged her shoulders downward so that she wanted to melt into the hard white slab in front of her. "David and I talked about it: If we were ever in real physical danger, like a fire or something, the kids were the priority. He'd get them out first. Or I would. The two of us, we were lower priority. I could go on, if I knew Victoria had died, but didn't know about him.... I could go on, not knowing where he was. But not knowing about her…"

The bunker was filled with a soft, low hiss of electronics and, occasionally, the gurgle of the baby noisily drinking.

"Any way to access her house without ringing the bells?" Mike asked.

"Don't try it," Thomas said, straightening up in the chair, alarmed. "You can only read into their files, listen in on their conversations. You can't interact with anything. We'd be positioned instantly. They won't stop for a cross then."

Mike tapped steadily, the noise ticking in Catherine's ears like an old pocket watch, taunting her with a reminder of time passing. She raised her head and glared at Mike, to her confusion, then at the fingers on the relay, and Mike jerked her hand away. "Sorry."

"Have there been any notices about any of us?" Connor asked Thomas.

"What do you think? You're William Connor. You'd usually be *doing* the notices. Of course they've mentioned you."

"We saw them, Will," Ruth reminded him.

"And then there's me," Mike said.

"I could try to contact somebody else in the family of one of Victoria's friends."

"Not from here," Thomas insisted.

Mike absent-mindedly resumed the tapping on the relay. The

screen burped again, a name added somewhere that repositioned all the others. Catherine stood up. "Stop that damned racket."

Again Mike jerked her fingers away, holding both hands in front of her as if to fend off harm. Then she whirled to glare at the relay, turned back to Catherine, fished into the shallow pocket of Catherine's dark, oversized pants and, pointing the tiny pager at the oval dish, pressed the key that sent a blizzard of minute lights sparkling across its void, then a short string of numbers: degrees, minutes, seconds.

Latitude N 37.1
Longitude W 77
Wind Speed 29 knots

i

LATE AFTERNOON shadows crept over the cement apron around the fuel station. Catherine paced between the open hood of the van and the door to peer past vinyl strips Thomas had fixed over the window there. Mike, holding a brilliant, thin shaft of the portable light down into the guts of the ancient van, glanced up from time to time to observe the pacing but suppressed comments.

With exquisite precision Connor touched the tiny wire enlarged into a cord under a magnifier he grasped with his other hand. "This is the one?"

"That's it." Thomas rested his elbows on the edge of the van's open mouth. "But you can't disconnect it, either."

"Damn!" Connor laid down the magnifier and ran his fingers through his hair. "If you can't take out the chip or the transmitter, and you can't disconnect the wire, why the hell am I looking at it?"

Thomas grinned. "You're not thinking."

Mike frowned in concentration and kept her eyes on the old man. After a moment she spoke: "Silicon. Want to mess it up just enough so it'll distort the signal through the transmitter. But not so much it'll set off the sequence to shut down the engine. Something very basic. Crude, even." She tapped the beacon in the palm of her left hand, glanced around the walls of the cubicle, squinting in the gloom. "Something simple. Dust..." She scurried past Catherine, who stood near Ruth, Virginia asleep in her arms. "Dust. Or acid."

Thomas snickered.

"That's you all over, Mike. Acid."

"Shut up, Connor. Won't take much. Got some old power packs around you haven't recycled, Thomas?"

The two of them bent over a heap of small, dirty cubes piled up in a carton and began sorting them. Shaking his head, Connor leaned his arms wearily over the edge of the van. Catherine approached to give him a large flask of water.

"Maybe we ought to just risk it."

He guzzled the drink and wiped his mouth on the navy sleeve.

"We won't have any choice. I never heard of any way to disable the positioning transmitter."

"If anybody would know, I guess you would," she said.

"You get after a particular interview, you think about things like that. Competing broadcasters getting there before you."

"Just anybody could tap into the positioning satellites?"

"Hell, yes, Catherine." He returned the flask to her. "We're complacent about it. We all abused these things, but would envireng do it? Oh, certainly not. Not that ethical authority. Hell, yes, Catherine. There're ways to tap into the satellites, if you got the equipment."

Thomas and Mike returned to the van brandishing a minuscule power pack and a piece of glass tube. Thomas slapped Mike's back. "All we got to do is transfer just the tiniest drop, the weest little bit onto the edge of the chip—"

"Where the transmitter wire's attached," Mike added. "It might misread, take it as nothing more than corrosion."

"And if it doesn't, and just shuts everything down?"

She shrugged. "Whatever you got for a Plan B."

"And you're going to aspirate the acid with that," he said incredulously.

"God's sake, Newsman, it'll be a speck. Not like I'm going to fill my mouth and spit fire or anything."

"Oh, give it here." He took the power pack from her. She shrugged again, Catherine thought perhaps with relief, and with her forefinger held the minute cube down as he cautiously scraped the corroded base of the pack and, after a sickly sheepish glance at them, sucked gently through the makeshift pipette. The end of the glass tube presently gleamed with a drop of yellowish-white material that he held with delicacy over the engine, motioning energetically with his free hand. Thomas scrambled forward with the magnifier and Catherine gently straightened the wire from the transmitter outward. Cursing profoundly, Connor tapped the top edge of the tube with the softest of touches until a speck of the yellow matter lay where he wanted it on the electronic device in the engine.

"Water?" Mike asked.

"Not necessary." Thomas shook his head. "Just give it time. Let it sit there. Get everything else ready, and we'll see."

Mike glanced once more toward Catherine.

Aware of the surreptitious looks her way, Catherine said she'd repack the vehicle with the few things they'd brought from Ruth's apartment. An almost resigned silence followed these words; she knew Connor's determination to help her carry out the new plan they had half-developed with only sketchy detail was equaled by Mike's increasing agitation as late afternoon approached. Mike had offered her opinion in a more tactful way than she usually did that retracing steps they'd already made wasn't very smart. Then, as Connor cleared his throat meaningfully, she'd looked up at him and said nothing else.

But she tapped her fingers against the seat she'd chosen near Ruth's, tapped faster and louder. The irritating click filled the cavernous cubicle and provoked Catherine to make loud noises to drown it out from time to time as she stored the assorted bundles again.

Thomas had opened the small white cube and brought out bottled juices and drinks for them to take with them, to buy time— he chuckled at this chestnut of a joke—and get them further up the road before they would have to stop again. They looked thirstily at the drinks but stored all but one in the van, opening that one for Virginia. Catherine had been trying to ignore a question arising in some primitive, anxious part of her brain, a question about that thirst, and, just as Connor had hypothesized his theories in his mother's house, she too had suspicions that were becoming conclusions. She ignored the nervous, agitated glances from Mike. Finding Victoria was even more important now than it had been before.

"I'll be back in a few minutes," Thomas said in the gloomy quiet. They stopped their various activities for a moment. He fiddled clumsily with the keypad. "Willie, I may need you—" a remark Catherine thought contrived—and when Connor rejoined them a moment later, they watched Thomas disappear into the locked passageway. He was back again in ten minutes, coding the keypad once more, and stood away from them. Mike leaped from the chair with purpose, Ruth gently laid Virginia's head upon her shoulder and rose also; Connor sighed once and went to the van.

Thomas cleared his throat. "It's set up. They'll wait until seven o'clock. When that's done, you'll need to leave, hit the route we plotted. Don't do a thing that'd attract envireng's attention on the way. Nothing. Don't exceed limits. Don't stop for food, make do with what you already got. If the transmitter's been disabled, or if you're real lucky and it's sending out an error signal, you got a little extra time."

"Before they figure out we're heading for Canada and start trying to locate Catherine's people."

"Fuel?" Mike raised her brows.

"Done. Shouldn't need more than two stops. Go where I marked." He shoved a fragile, brittle sheaf of papers at Connor.

"Don't know when I've seen a map," Connor mumbled, carefully opening folded sections.

"Told you *I'd* help," Mike sniffed.

"Don't get your feelings hurt," the old man patted her shoulder. "The less you know about my place here, the better, for you."

"And you," she said with irony.

"And me," he agreed.

Ruth passed Virginia to Catherine and eased into the back seat of the van again. Thomas reached out awkwardly toward her with a crooked claw of a hand, and they looked at each other a moment. Catherine passed by him, tapped his back.

"Why don't you come with us? They'll know we came here. They'll be here themselves sometime soon."

He shook his head. "This's my place. Couldn't stand to think of it being taken apart. Which is what'd happen if I went missing." He chuckled. "They'll ask, oh, yeah, they'll ask if I saw all of you, since you've already been traced this far. I'll tell 'em I don't know, I was in my shelter the way I was supposed to be. The way they ordered me to be. They'll want to look around. I'll have to let 'em. But my scarecrow'll make them stop, for a while, anyway."

"Do they suspect..." Connor asked haltingly. "You do things like this often?"

Thomas grinned. "Why do you think I even have a scarecrow?"

"You ought to come with us."

"Oh, they'll wonder. What the hell. They'll get even with me in about eight months anyway. They figure they can wait. Now get on the road. Keep your curious nose out of things," he said to Mike. "Too damned nosy."

"You old peddler," she shot back, and he cackled at the insult.

They could have stayed there for a long time, artificially comfortable in the cocooning fuel cubicle with its high ceiling and dim corners—all except Catherine, whose mind was occupied with the excruciating problem of risking Virginia's life to save Victoria's. There was nothing else to say to Thomas; they sat mutely for a moment until he swung the passenger door shut and, after checking outside, pressed buttons to open the large cubicle gate. Connor took a deep breath and put his finger into the switchlock. The motor began with an odd whir that frightened them, the display scrolling off a warning about possible contaminants in the engine block, reminding them a service check was required sometime during the next week, and then the sound smoothed itself out.

"Good, old-fashioned gunk," Mike said.

"Still don't know what it's transmitting. Or *whether*."

"Quit thinking about it. He knew what he was doing about that, anyway. It's the least of our worries now." She glanced backward at Catherine and settled deep into her seat. "We got much bigger worries."

He turned slowly and gave her the cold, steady look again. She shifted her shoulders a little, twitched, resumed tapping her nails.

The sun at their left, they headed north, avoiding the electromag again, staying on decayed byways Connor and Ruth seemed to know by memory. Most of the rainwater had soaked into the parched ground, except in swampy areas and uneven ditches, where it lay in pools no longer reflecting iridescence but an eerie pink tinge that Mike appeared interested in, craning her neck to look at them as they eased past. The roads Thomas had picked were ancient, even more so than the one they'd driven on yesterday morning, pavement abruptly giving way to mud, where trees overshadowed the lane, and drying dirt, wherever there'd been adequate sunshine that day. Vacant spots indicated old house sites, the houses themselves long gone, perhaps razed, perhaps moved. Catherine, immersed for so many years in the life back home, David's work, Victoria's school, their compact community of friends about their own age, had forgotten these places, from which her mother and father and grandfather had fled years earlier. Her mouth became a straight, grim line when she saw the bright-orange "Condemned" sign on the only building they encountered beside that road, a ramshackle wooden store long since abandoned.

"I'll never see my house again."

Connor shrugged. "You might."

"No, I won't. We left my home behind yesterday when we

escaped to Columbia, then we went to the university, no shelter there, right, and even Ruth said their stackhouse wasn't a home...."

"It wasn't."

"And now, here we are, going away from my town for the second time. I'll never see my house again."

The tapping noise from the front right seat increased in tempo.

The quiet was sad and oppressive. She sighed, changed the subject. "Connor told us he grew up not far from here. How long ago was the area populated?"

"It's been a while," Ruth said. "The urbanization trend—"

"More efficient, for us all to live closer," Connor interrupted.

Mike turned on him. "You're sarcastic about that, now. Yesterday, you weren't. You really believed it."

"But nobody made us."

"What are we going to do when we finally get to campus?" Mike said plaintively. "What about authority? You know they'll be there, trying to control unrest, they'll have checkpoints...."

"We could find out. Want more information?" Connor said. There was silence.

They had activated one of the screens in Thomas's listening room earlier, to glean the scraps of knowledge envireng was allowing on the free airways. Thomas then tapped into the secure line, and in terror they had read scrolling bulletins detailing areas that had been searched already for the fugitives, who were now identified, all four of them, as probable murderers driven insane by a partial, late exposure to Eutopix as the chemical was losing its most lethal power. "Not just killers, but insane killers. That'll keep everybody off the streets, make *us* just that much more prominent," Connor had said. Then, as Mike stared at her own name, mentioned frequently in the dispatches, he'd added, "Oh, and they're being honest again. No attempts to hide that it was the Eutopix."

"How would they ever hide something like that?" Ruth asked.

He'd given her a look of disgust.

Authority knew about the envireng and the tech in his dull navy who'd used his charge gun on Theo before Connor had leaped upon him, and they knew about David and Catherine Millen's baby, and the older daughter who remained missing, possibly to rejoin her mother, one of the small band of outlaws. They knew about Ruth, who had not been located, either. They'd carefully searched the rifled apartment on campus, cross-checked the occupants' account inventory, had a description of the clothing removed from the premises. It had been determined from infrared scans and disturbances recorded in the electromag strips during the previous night that the individuals had made their way from the campus to Columbia, where, in the apartment of the parents of the broadcaster, the violence had occurred. Psyphi experts analyzing and interpreting the situation had determined there was a probability the individuals were still in Columbia, it being unlikely they'd succeeded in crossing earlier roadblocks.

Connor had scoffed at that. "Murderers, and crazy, and too stupid to slip through their little knots. Well, at least we have that one advantage."

"Or think we do," Mike had commented, her eyes on the screen. "Can't be sure everything we see here is everything they know."

Avoiding the town today meant following a wide, semicircular path east of the electromag. For miles the van bounced and jolted along dirt lanes interspersed with stretches of pavement where envireng had not found it essential to destroy the old roads or had just run out of resources before accomplishing that objective. The sun began to stream through the glass on the left side of the vehicle. Catherine found herself patting one foot in time to Mike's agitated rhythm.

They had consumed an hour in what would have been a half-hour journey on the electromag. The final stretch, marked with a pencil in Thomas's wobbly hand, led them at last to a road in better condition than the ones they'd been on, and to one more lump of dirt, a mound they saw from a distance glowing reddish orange like a volcano with lava streaming down its sides. Connor sucked in another slow breath; Mike glared at the obstacle.

On the other side lay the unavoidable encounter with strips that would become aware of their presence, monitoring their actions and speed and path.

Connor stopped, and they gazed as if hypnotized.

"Beek," Virginia said tentatively, and Catherine handed her a flask of water.

"This is it. Here's where we decide if we're going on or not. Where we risk ourselves to find Catherine's daughter. Who might not even be where we think anyway. Nobody knows if she made all the connections on time."

"Shut up, Mike," Connor said pleasantly. "I told you a long way up the road to get out then or hold your tongue. We have to think. So be useful. You seem to know a lot we don't. Do the strips register a vehicle the same way they do animals?"

"No."

"Why not?"

"Well, you have the speed variable, for one thing. Animals usually contact the strips a fraction of a second longer. Vehicles touch maybe for a millisecond. And in lines parallel to the strips. Animals don't do that. They just try to cross the road. At right angles, now, you know. You even said it yourself."

"The damned things and their stupid little minds... So, all right, we cross the edge slowly, and at right angles, the monitors won't pick us up?"

Mike turned to look disbelievingly at him. "What do you think? Think they haven't been wired to know the difference? Elementary Programming, first year."

"Let's do it, anyway," Catherine said. Mike twisted around in the seat to stare at her now. "You used acid to try something Connor said wasn't possible."

"Which may not have worked," he pointed out. "Envireng may have been monitoring us all the way, letting us get out of the backwoods before they pounced, make their job easier."

"But they haven't yet," she said, "and, anyway, what's the difference? If we trip the alarms, it won't matter. If doing it at right angles, slowly, might get us over without being caught, we should try that."

Mike squeezed her eyes shut and waved fists in the air. Connor laughed and engaged the motor, creeping around the lump of earth and to the edge of the strips. "The shock," he warned, and they gritted their teeth at the mild electricity that poured through them. Catherine clasped Virginia tightly. The baby's eyes were wide, her wispy hair on end.

After the shock was done, they found themselves perpendicular to the sides of the highway, beached like a whale. "Now I'll demonstrate subtlety," Connor said, beginning a back-and-forth process of turning the van northward again without brushing against the strips. Mike tapped her fingers and glanced up and down the road as he toiled. Catherine waited, her eyes gazing out the front window.

They were on campus.

ii

CONNOR PRESSED buttons to find the frequency of the broadcast Thomas had told them to listen to, and eased on up the road. The van was filled with edgy voices now, announcers repeating bulletins about hospitals and shelter unsealings, giving advice about how to purify a contaminated water supply. There were more vehicles; occasionally they met one going south, and two eventually turned up behind them, at the regulated distance. Catherine suggested the time had come for them to duck down, an idea Ruth agreed with. She unharnessed herself and sat on the floor with Virginia, and the two of them played at some fingercounting game Catherine did not understand. She watched them uncomprehendingly, then eased down behind Connor's seat, her eyes resting momentarily on the brassy tint of his hair. She opened the nearest soft bundle and pawed through the odd clothing Ruth had brought along until she found a length of bright-colored towel. Rising to her knees, she wrapped it around Connor's head from behind. "You need to get down, too," she told Mike before sinking back to the floor.

"I don't want a surprise, like we had on campus yesterday," Mike said grimly.

"With Will seemingly the only person in the van, we'll attract less attention, dear."

Mike tapped her fingers.

"You know this was one of Thomas's conditions. Nobody but me to see where we were to go. Just in case."

"In case we were all caught in the trap we're walking into."

"No, so only one of us could betray anybody else," he told her bluntly. "Get down. We all agreed. I'll tell you when I need your help."

Groaning, she slid downward, her eyes level with the bottom of the windows until Connor pushed her head and she sat flat on the bottom of the van.

"So how's it feel to be totally out of personal control?" he asked, and she pinched his leg and twisted.

They could feel from the steady hum of the engine that Connor drove with the kind of consistency envireng praised. Sometimes it seemed to them that the road took sharp curves left or right, and sometimes the curves came constantly, bewildering any sense of direction they had, and their eyes met with unspoken anxiety.

The vehicle slowed. Alongside the lanes, shallow piles of litter lay sodden and vaguely misty against obstacles they had been blown against by the previous day's howling wind, but only Connor saw this. Consulting the map more frequently, he turned down streets of student housing until suddenly he halted with a jolt that brought Mike up again.

Catherine lifted her head cautiously. They were at the rear of a row of gloomy, austere apartments not unlike the stackhouse Ruth had lived in, hidden partly by a group of heavy shrubs. "Fifth," Connor said. He eased the van down the row, so that its right side was near the door of the apartment, and got out, self-consciously touching the turban Catherine had contrived for him, pressed the ID panel beside the door. The door opened a little; they saw a face inside as Connor spoke and gesticulated once or twice at the van. The face was thrust outward, assessing them, counting, and Connor returned.

"Quick, and one at a time."

"Why do we all have to go in?" Mike objected. "Whyn't they just bring the kid out?"

A grin on his face, he wrenched her from the front seat and marched her rapidly inside. "That was mean," Catherine whispered as he reached next for her.

"Oh, maybe she'll enjoy exchanging rebel news with them for a while," and with a glance up and down the row, he shoved her inside next, Virginia clinging to her.

When he and Ruth had dashed safely inside the building, the four adults lined up against a wall, flinching under the suspicious eyes of two wiry-haired youths.

"William Connor, Catherine; my mother; Mike, and the baby is Virginia."

"Aren't you polite. We don't give our names out."

"Where's my daughter?" Catherine said over him.

"Thought there would be only four." The nearer of the two students scanned their faces, back and forth.

"Four adults."

"He said only four."

Catherine heaved a sigh. "Maybe he forgot Virginia—I don't

know; he's old. Does it matter? Where's my daughter? Victoria! Are you here?"

The first student glowered at Connor as the second one nodded and left the room. Catherine started to follow, only to be barred from the hallway.

"You don't have to see everything," he said. She shrank away for a moment, then shoved him aside as a skinny kid with emu-feather hair was escorted into her sight hauling a lumpy school-issue tote.

Victoria submitted to a frantic embrace, clutched Catherine's arms with thin fingers. "Where've you been?"

"Here and there, up and down the road…" She heard Connor laughing softly behind her. "Where've *you* been?"

"With Rosalind."

"Rosalind?"

"Yeah, Mom, second-quadrant," she said with a hint of the usual sarcasm.

"You skipped school yesterday?"

Victoria pulled back at the tone, and they both laughed, and heard the others lining the wall join in, and even the students snickered.

"I told you I didn't want to go. Crazy thing to make anybody do."

"You stayed with Rosalind."

She evaded: "Not really."

"What'd you do?"

"We sort of went to Columbia for the day."

"Columbia?"

"Yeah. After the announcements, and the alarms, we got into one of the shelters there." She leaned back away, gazing at Catherine's face, tentatively stroked the darker hair.

"What happened to *you*? You're yellow." Wrenching free, she stood back and looked at the others. "You're all yellow."

"You, on the other hand, are out of fashion," Mike said coldly. "Bleaching was passé a year ago."

"Who's she?" Victoria touched one of the feathery wisps.

"A friend of your mother's," Mike said.

"I don't remember—"

"Connor, we have to go."

The first student shook his head. "Not yet."

Catherine wondered if he was demanding ransom for their freedom. Mike's hand curved reflexively into the shape of the charge gun, which she had left in the van.

"You can't leave yet. They've been monitoring you about ten minutes."

"Told you," Mike whispered.

"They probably wanted to get you all at one time, in one place, and some of us too."

"How do you know?"

"Your old friend's not the only person who can listen in. They picked you up at the electromag. Followed you in. But they've been confused about the signal. They weren't able to do anything but visually monitor you, pass word on to the next security."

"We're trapped here? We won't get out?" Catherine said.

"Not yet. Just wait." He gestured at chairs behind him. "Rest for a while."

"We should leave *now*—" Mike made fists again and sat down.

"You're getting better at self-control." Connor took a seat beside her. "Do what he says. Take a rest. Thomas worked it all out."

"Where's Dad?" Victoria asked.

Catherine had wanted to avoid that question until they were somewhere on the road again. Virginia clamored for Victoria to hold her, and, grateful for the distraction, Catherine let the child crawl up on her sister.

"He going to meet us somewhere else?"

She drew a heavy breath, tried to find words.

"At home?" Victoria continued, a tremolo in her voice.

Catherine looked away. Victoria moved nearer and sat cold and hard as a gargoyle, her face twisted into a blank, frozen expression of nothing. The baby patted her and played with the wafting hair that tickled her nose from time to time as the climate system blew fresh air at them. Catherine gazed at a metallic poster dangling precariously from a nail on the wall opposite her. *Economy*, it read above an artistic rendering of a public transport and smiling passengers, and, at the bottom and obviously graffitied by one of the inhabitants of the apartment, *of the brain*.

Connor left his chair to run two cupfuls of water from the dispenser and gave one to Victoria.

"I'm not thirsty."

"Your sister is."

"How would *you* know?" she asked.

He shrugged. Victoria held the cup to the baby's mouth, and Virginia gulped as quickly as Connor downed his own. "How long?" he asked amiably.

The first student started to say something, when Mike interrupted: "What's going on? I don't know why we can't all know."

"Shut up," Connor told her. "Be patient."

"Who's she?"

"My niece. Sister's child. Hot-tempered. Short attention span." Connor seemed to study her under partly closed eyes. "Working on self-control."

The student stared at her face, turned back to Connor as if to say more, when a low, dull thud rattled the metallic poster. It hung trembling a brief moment before crashing to the floor after a second and then a third noise, both louder. Mike leaped up. "What was that?"

"Wait." The students listened intently at the door. A sudden, clangorous cycling scream commenced quite near the apartment, wailing more faintly as it fled away, followed by another shriek not very far off.

"Now leave," the first student calmly ordered.

Connor nodded. "Out, out, out," and he turned quickly to Catherine and his mother, grasping Victoria's elbow and shoving her ahead of him. Mike scampered behind them all, her eyes apprehensive as she passed the students who guarded the back courtyard now with strangely-adapted charge guns. Connor harnessed himself in and, engaging the motor, followed the gestures of the students, who directed him to go right at the end of the drive and return to the main electromag.

"Shouldn't we—" Catherine stopped.

"What? Tell 'em thanks?" Connor looked briefly left, then pulled away from the apartment row. "Thomas did that already. Besides, they owed him. —He said," he added hastily.

It was past twilight now, but he forced the van's lamps to stay unlit until they were safely off campus. Mike commented on this with sarcasm: "They know how to find us, with or without lights, you know," but no one responded. Catherine was thirsty and wished she'd satisfied that need in the students' housing, as

Connor had; she determined now not to use any more of their water than she had to.

"Where're we going?" Victoria asked plaintively.

"I assume," Connor mused, "they only monitored our approximate movements; I assume they may not know exactly what kind of thing we're in—"

"They knew all about Ruth and Theo. That's a stupid assumption," Mike remarked.

"Nevertheless, one I'm making, so I can go to the next step. Call it a fond hope. I'm assuming lots of things. I'm also assuming the positioner's still misregistering. Thomas left the route from campus open-ended, except for fueling stops here—" he pointed at something on the ancient paper— "in West Virginia, and here—" another jab— "in Pennsylvania. When we reach the international border, there may be another distraction. We'll see. Don't know exactly what Thomas arranged." With a quick glance at him, Catherine saw he was lying.

"We're going into Canada?" Victoria asked.

"We're going to try our damnedest."

"So you're staying on the electromag?" Catherine asked him.

"Oh, yeah. The busiest routes I can find, most congested... Try to blend in. If ever there was a time we needed to be just another van going up a road, it's now."

iii

COLUMBIA LAY far behind them, an intellectual outpost in the darkness. Victoria slumped upon the seat behind Catherine clasping Virginia beside her; and as Catherine glanced through the dim at the two gently snoring sisters, she wondered whether Victoria, like her, had passed the previous night in the company of sleepless acquaintances, pondering the fate of the rest of the family. She ran her tongue over dry lips, shook her head in frustration.

"Pour me some water," she told Ruth softly. "Half a cup."

She drained the full container she was given, then rolled it around and around on her leg. "I worry about what's going to happen to us." She spoke a little louder, so Connor could hear.

"One thing at a time. First we have to get to the border."

"I mean later. Much later," she added, as he began saying something about broadcasts. "I mean, what's this stuff done to us?"

The silence after this question frightened her. She rummaged beneath the seat until she felt the smooth metal of the portable beacon against her hand and turned the light for an instant on the two dozing girls, the older one resting in her own feathery white pillow and the baby a bundle beside her. Even Connor raised his eyes quickly to the mirror.

"Look at them. Will Victoria outlive Virginia? What if—" she turned the beacon off, grappling for other words less terrifying— "what if that stuff didn't just speed up cell activity—we know it did that—wouldn't it speed up ageing, cause mutations, new types of cancer? What if our lives have been shortened?"

Mike tapped her fingers frantically and shifted her shoulders.

"How much would they be shortened? Is there a way to put a number on how fast we've been accelerated? And from there, how long we might have?"

Connor's eyes were steady on the road, his brows held in a deep frown.

"You ask too many questions," Mike said bluntly. "We can't stand it right now."

"You have only yourself to be concerned for," she pointed out.

She waited for a response and, getting none, went back to rolling the glass around again, unconsciously working it into a rhythm to accompany the nervous tapping in the front. The electromag was moderately busy tonight, transports and poolvans herded along at regulated distances and speeds, just so close and no more, just so fast and no more. As they neared the ubiquitous energy-conscious road signs, these turned on at the proper intervals to inform them of other roads and towns, turned off as they passed. Victoria sighed deeply once in her sleep, and Ruth leaned over to pat her.

Kilometers grew behind them. The next sign instructed them that Lynchburg was four kilometers ahead.

The tapping in the front seat abruptly stopped. Mike wriggled her shoulders two or three times and slid her legs sideways into the aisle to look at Ruth and Catherine, a purposeful, grim expression on her face.

"I'll be leaving in Lynchburg. I'm a dangerous person for you to have along. Envireng might let you all slip out just to stop publicity. But they really won't just let me go."

"I told you she was lying," Connor remarked amiably.

"I never lied," she said. Catherine heard a soft rustling in the seat behind her. "I didn't lie. I just didn't—"

"—tell the truth," he supplied.

"I told you what I could."

"Don't believe you. Why would envireng be after you for anything but that disaster yesterday morning? You could rightfully claim that as a mistake, a miscalculation; they'd punish you a little and let you off."

"To be in a study."

"But that's the rest of us, too. Yet you keep telling us you're dangerous, we shouldn't be with you, they're after you."

She sat with arms stiffly at her side, gripping the seat as if she thought she might be ejected.

"You know how the chemical went missing. You know who got it."

It was a statement he made, not a question, the beginning of a cross-examination in a trial. Quiet, emphatic, no doubt. Catherine hadn't thought of the possibility.

"So just tell us. You're not going anywhere right now."

An ominous quiet filled the van like a cold, ghostly draft raising prickles on their skin.

"I *will* tell you. Maybe you can tell somebody else when I leave. So, they tried to trace it down. It wasn't gone all at once, but over a long period of time. They suspected Franklin— he'd been in the chemlabs a lot because of the iodide, the neptunium; he would've been able to siphon some off a little at a time, peddle it to insurgents, buy himself some special things."

"Did he? I'm sure you know." Connor raised his voice a little.

In her mind Catherine saw the ring glinting on the finger yesterday morning. Who wore flashy rings these days? Nobody she knew; they were a waste, an extravagance. She remembered the gleam, remembered the annoyance at having Mike and him with her in the poolvan she and David had been so frugal, so economical, so responsible, to be allowed to purchase on sanction loan.

"He was one. But he didn't have time to get the amount that was gone, not just himself. Two in my department suddenly took these holidays to Mexico—they said relatives there had sent them coupons and transportation tickets."

"I bet you got some of it, too, didn't you. Used it for a few 'special things' of your own."

It was a sneering, challenging sort of comment that chilled Catherine, an accusation she hadn't wanted to voice. Ruth murmured, "Will."

"I told you already: Envireng fixed me and my family up. I wouldn't have needed it."

The shiver began at Catherine's knees and travelled up her spine before reversing back down. *Who cares about sunsets?*

"Those insurgents on campus knew of you. Maybe they were your friends once. Maybe you passed some of the stuff on to whoever was in that plane—was that person one of the group?" Connor's voice grew louder, filled the van.

Catherine took in the wide-eyed glance Mike—still sideways in her seat—turned to her and Ruth. "He wasn't anybody I—" She stopped.

"Ah. You were in on the whole plot. How much did you give them? I guess that's why you knew you hadn't made the dome strong enough, right."

"No—I had no access to the stuff—"

"That's why you want to leave us." Connor was inexorable, loud. Catherine recalled the awards at the elder stackhouse: "Investigative Reporting Excellence." Connor's interviews on broadcasts were sometimes brutal; David had found them amusing. *He's not even a lawyer. Look up his background: He doesn't have any specific technical knowledge in any one field; he just has a nice face, puts on a good show. Knows how to extract things from people.*

She'd wondered if it was scorn or admiration in David's voice.

"Envireng'll ask us about you, then let us go, or at least maintain us in comfort," Connor went on. "It's you they'll put somewhere, interrogate, punish, because you worked with the dissidents and planned everything out."

If you did that, I'll strangle you myself long before envireng gets you.

Connor went quiet and turned his head to gape at her, Ruth gasped softly, and she realized she'd said it aloud.

Mike's hands clutched at her seat; she looked back and forth from Catherine and Ruth to Connor. "I only found out somebody'd sold a lot of the stuff to them, they'd fooled around with it, added biotes to it—they had a plan on the table, I'd figured *that* out by myself—"

"How? You still in the group? Still know their codes?"

"No! I wondered about Franklin, yes, that jackass, and I did uncode those Eutopix files, saw how much had disappeared, asked—" She stopped, sucked in a breath.

"So you *are* still in the group."

A heavy, foreboding silence settled over them. Mike let go of the seat and fisted and unfisted her hands. "No." It was much quieter than before; she shook her head. "But their secrets aren't coded as well as they think they are. So you know you're 'in' when you find that symbol on things. You know which one—that hexagon, the thing on that plane; you noticed it yourself. I'd draw it on my compcorder case at university. Had a pendant on a cord, wore it under my shirt while I was there. How dumb can you get," she scoffed.

"Tattoos? You look like a person who'd have tattoos." Another loud gibe from Connor, biting.

"You know how people feel about tattoos these days."

"Same way they do about nicknames."

Ruth said, "Shh."

"So I found one of the idiots'd started putting extra stuff into the Eutopix he'd managed to get. File was last accessed four days ago. What a fool." Her voice grew softer. "I'm not lying."

"Yeah, I think you're not, now. So, what do you mean, 'extra stuff'? You've said that more than once."

Catherine, watching her, knew the answer would be bad even before Mike shut her eyes and grimaced. "He got hold of some Ebola from Asia. Threw it in, just in case that old Eutopix didn't do its thing with blood vessels anymore. Though it probably would've, mixed up with neptunium ions. Then," and she hesitated again, a deep breath, "one of the few things that fool did of any value, he discovered what turns on the progeria gene."

"What is that?"

Connor answered Ruth: "It's a non-hereditary mutation that speeds up ageing." As they computed the significance of that, he added, "I did a report on it a long time ago."

"I'm not lying." This time it was a request for them to believe her.

"I know journalists in Canada. I could get this on today, tomorrow. It'd save all our necks, even yours. I assume you have proof."

"Proof?" She laughed. "I copied everything, re-codelocked those pages, hid them in my own files this week. But all the alarms on their grid go off when they've been hacked into, even if they can't find out what was snooped on. There's always a tag left. So they know I left the safe net and tapped in."

"But you'd been given access to those documents about the Eutopix. They wouldn't find it unusual for you to go in and look…" Catherine paused.

"That's not why they'd be after me."

"The other work. The things added in." Even Ruth figured it out.

"Oh, they may already have that fool that did those off-the-record experiments. Probably do. But he may have them stored where they'll never be found. And, then, I did have connections to the group. And I'm good at snooping; they know that now. They'll never get into *my* files, but then, neither will I," and her voice dropped. "I could go to the nearest grid station, maybe in Lynchburg here, and tap in and bring it up. Save it somewhere else. They might've even left my codes alone, so I *could* do that, so they could catch me." She fisted, unfisted her hands. "Thomas, he did all right at Columbia, but campuses are surely boiling by now because of what happened yesterday and today, without any help from him. Students have nothing but contempt for envireng."

"Except you," he said, smiling coldly.

"I told you, they know how to make you do what they want. I'll never get to my documents. But they tagged every file that went through the system. If I downloaded them, they'd have me just like that positioner—" she motioned toward the front of the vehicle— "is going to help them find us. And so," she continued, breathing heavily, "I have to try to link back up with the students. I'll plant hints into the net that I'm still in the country; maybe they'll stop thinking about the rest of you."

"You won't be safe," Catherine said. "Somebody'd eventually turn you over to them."

Haven't we taught her ethics and responsibility? The shiver went up and down again.

"Or maybe you just want out before we are stopped. Maybe you're trying to save your own skin."

She gave Connor a sour smile. "It's time for me to leave. I

couldn't keep going with you, no matter what; we'll kill each other before much longer."

"I tell you what. You're not going to leave us now. What's gonna happen is, I'll take you to the border and march you into a station and hand you over to envireng myself; at least Catherine and her children and Mother may get away."

"You wouldn't do that. I know."

"Watch me." He nodded, clenching the steering mechanism, gripping it and squeezing. "I'll see to it it's done big, public. You can tell your story, and maybe somebody'll feel sorry for you—"

He shrugged off a tentative, almost gentle punch she aimed at his shoulder, and another, harder one, and then held the steering mechanism with one hand and used the other to grasp the black curls and jerk her head back and forth. Ruth shrieked for them to stop, leaned forward, stretching arms out in an attempt to separate them. A noise behind her, and Catherine turned to see Victoria sitting up, watching the battle, the bleached plumage wafting about her face. With a mighty tug she hauled the tote out from underneath the seat.

"Don't even think it—" Catherine warned her.

She ripped the tight-fix fasteners apart that held together the largest compartment. The noise was a loud scratch, like an enormous swath of fabric being torn in two, and it froze the man and girl at the front. Her lips curled in disgust, Victoria pulled out her school-issue compcorder, opened it, and tapped. She sat back as the screen filled with print.

"You didn't do it right. I *did*," she said coldly.

Latitude N 38
Longitude W 75.4
Wind Speed 30 knots

i

THE BROADCASTS they picked up from Canada said the province they drove toward was enjoying lovely, crisp autumn weather now, the hurricane far away, following its predicted path to the northeast, leaving the United States and returning to its ocean spawning ground after being wrung of its moisture. The poolvan sped onward, the five adults inside having stopped paying attention to the gentle reminders that scrolled occasionally across the panel to inform them of a minor malfunction in the engine area that needed servicing.

The women clustered together in the rear, reading Victoria's stolen files. Because she still regarded Mike with resentful suspicion, she kept the compcorder an arm's length away, frowning each time Mike muttered, "*Diabhalta*," at some sections. Connor objected and ordered them to read or at least summarize the documents aloud.

"You found all of this on your own." Mike was for once awed.

Victoria shrugged. "They told us to research everything we could. I figured out a way to get more than everybody else. So. That was why they wanted me to uncode my compcorder. So they could see what I'd got. I was too scared to be there yesterday, Mom."

"Vindicated," Mike said rather calmly, a grim smile stretching her face, making her seem younger than ever. "Everything I told you. It's here. The missing amounts, the things they thought they'd covered up so well..."

"Victoria." Catherine hesitated, not sure she wanted the answer she was seeking. "Do you know...did you find out anything about particular people unreporting the Eutopix? Was there anything about that?"

The girl frowned into the slowly scrolling screen Mike was reading from.

"The workers that sold it. Mike said she thought Franklin did. Do you know who else?"

Victoria shrugged and didn't meet her eyes.

As Catherine was framing another question, Mike reached forward and pressed a hasty sequence of keys. Startled, Victoria grabbed the compcorder and jerked it away.

"What're you doing?"

"I'm through. Need to save the power pack—"

"The power pack's fine. This's my machine. You have no business touching it."

"Take it easy." Mike held out her hands in front of her.

"You could erase it."

"I bet nobody can get through your passcodes."

"No, you can't. I'm the only one."

"And, anyway, think: I have no reason, none, to crash the file. I'd even fight old Connor up there—" she gestured— "if he tried to."

"Why the hell would I?" he complained.

"So, you see?"

Victoria, still distrustful, eased the computer back to her lap, at last removing her gaze from Mike and looking at the screen which was now frozen in place. Catherine leaned over to see what Mike had wanted to hide.

The page was incompletely displayed in the middle of a sentence: *—feel closure, relatives allowed to view victims purported to be dead, held in suspended state by implementation of paralytic agents. After grieving process completed, relatives ushered away, victims removed for further observation at—*

Seeing her mother's face change, Victoria twisted away, typing characters until the machine shut itself off. She closed the screen down with a snap, stuffed it back into the tote, looked away from Catherine.

"You didn't need to see that," Mike remarked.

"What? What didn't she need to see?"

"None of your concern Connor."

"What they did with some of the people they airdropped Eutopix on, in the drought," Catherine told him. "Let their family look at them, think they were dead, when they had them drugged to seem that way. Then—"

"Study 'em. Yeah. I told you that."

Connor winced and kept his eyes straight forward.

Victoria huddled away from Catherine, turning cold and

gargoyle-like again.

"He died," Mike said with assurance. "I tell you, nobody on site would've lived. He was out of it right then. That very instant."

"There were always rumors," Catherine spoke slowly. "Always, even when I was a girl. You know: Kept 'em in rooms, alive, let 'em wither away for years. But envireng always seemed to be so forthright about it."

"Envireng always had to tell what it couldn't control, couldn't manipulate," Mike said dryly. "If there's one thing to be grateful for, it's that since the twentieth century, things can't be hidden anymore. Too many people able to tap into a system, find it out. Like I did. Like she did—" she gestured at Victoria. "Of course they had to be forthright, about stuff they didn't have locked down in their own facilities." She shook her head. "Get it on the air, Connor. Campuses in turmoil like they are, and then this gets aired, envireng go down."

"To be replaced by what?"

She shrugged. "Couldn't be much worse."

"It has been."

"Stop preaching—you're not the same, we're all different. Anybody else get that? We're different now. We've killed people... None of us can claim being ethical again. Holy Mother, we've killed people. Hardly any murders any more. But we've done it. Us. We've done it."

"Had no choice—" He frowned at the words. "They'd've killed us—"

"Oh, no—they'd've just sedated us indefinitely. What did that cretin on campus say? Parasitized? We'd've been parasitized. But not killed. No. We've done the killing..." She shivered, her shoulders twitching again.

"You didn't care yesterday."

"And I still don't—not because of them; because of me. We're different."

"It's not the chemical," he said.

She tapped the fingers nervously, gazed out her window into the darkness. "But that's what they're saying: It drove us insane. Maybe it did. Anyway, I can't wait to see them wrung out, watch them trying to explain it away. Line 'em up, shove 'em off the cliff one by one. Listen to 'em scream as they go down." She glanced at Catherine. "What's wrong with you?"

"I just want to get out and get my girls out."

"You don't care about anything else?"

The anger in Mike's voice made Catherine tired. "Probably not about the same things you do. Somewhere since Columbia, I stopped." When the dreadful thoughts and doubts came, she might have added.

"Oh, you feel like you've achieved your goals, so now why care about anybody else."

"It's not that."

"Don't go crying on me again." She turned away in distaste.

"Shut up, Mike."

"Shut up, yourself, Connor Newsman. Quit telling me that."

When the sun began warming the right side of the old van, Virginia awoke and clambered into Catherine's arms, her eyes still heavy with sleep. "Beek?"

"How could she want anything now?" Victoria said with distaste, a reminder of how little she'd eat sometimes before leaving for school. Catherine watched concern dawn on Victoria's face. Ruth silently handed a container of juice to the girl, and she arranged it so Virginia could drink without spilling it on the makeshift tunic.

In the early moments before dawn, Connor had turned off the electromag along a route listed as a scenic tour. Peering at the ancient map, comparing it to the dimly-lit landscape, he finally stopped at a replica stop to refuel. The others remained silent in the van as a few words were exchanged outside; the owner of the fuel stop regarded them warily, nodded, completed the task and, with a lifted chin and a hint of stubborn satisfaction in his face, sent them onward. Connor was pleased at the van's low consumption of the fuel and dared to hope the journey might be finished without another stop. He didn't like stopping now, he said. If they were found, with the broadcasts reporting that everything was in uproar, envireng would blame them for sedition and treason, besides theft and murder.

"So this'll be my legacy," Ruth commented. "Theo would've loved it."

The electromag through the remainder of West Virginia and northward in Pennsylvania became more crowded with public transports and private poolvans maintaining a responsible speed and distance from one another. Connor pressed buttons occasionally to change channels from a Canadian station to one in Pittsburgh and then back. The voices were edgier now, more urgent, more campus unrest reported, casualty reports getting larger. They heard their own names sometimes, new sins attributed to them, including those Connor feared. His shoulders hunched, tense. They would make Buffalo by early evening. It would not be soon enough to suit him.

In northwestern Pennsylvania the van's brain suddenly stopped scrolling its polite warning about engine contaminants. They'd ignored it for so long that its absence went unnoticed for a while, and only Connor's furtive glances at last got Catherine's attention.

"What's wrong?"

He gestured.

"The chip rerouted itself," Mike whispered.

He shook his head. "I don't know. I don't think so—I imagine they finally got a fix on the van by its malfunction. They probably knew we were in Mother's vehicle, got its code, bounced a signal telling the positioner to shut off. Located the van by its return confirmation. I knew this couldn't last."

"What do we do now?" Catherine asked.

"Nothing to do but drive till they find us. Hope we get closer than we are now. It won't be long—" he did not finish the statement, and nobody asked what he meant.

Thirty-five kilometers south of Buffalo, the van hummed onward, its occupants engaged in entertaining the baby whose fretfulness increased at a pace equal to the growth of their own anxiety. Conversation died, Connor and Mike barely glancing at one another, Victoria composing abstract cartoons on the compcorder for Virginia's amusement, Ruth and Catherine contemplating losses and gains. The international border wouldn't be difficult to cross, Connor had explained somewhere in the early morning in Pennsylvania, because the country needed the Canadian market, and open borders were the condition Canada placed. Still, they'd be scanned at least perfunctorily; and, since envireng maintained a facility at each of the more important crossings to deal with the rare criminal, if they were apprehended, Connor told them softly, it would be fast. They'd be in authority custody before anybody even knew they were in that part of the country. The border wasn't a tape to burst through in victory but the ultimate hurdle an exhausted runner had to jump.

They all heard the shrill, cycling scream at the same time, but only Mike dared vocalize the thought: "No, not now. It's too close. It's not right, it's not fair…"

"Two behind," Connor said tersely. "One ahead." He gestured up the road where the third white authority van occupied the middle of the highway, an obstacle pacifically impelling them by its own lumbering pace to slow down.

"How far?" Ruth asked. "Run for it?"

His hands gripped the steering mechanism. He did not answer at first and Catherine, touched his shoulder. "Connor?"

"Too far. Close. But too far. Still too far inside the country."

"Don't leave this highway!" Mike shrieked. "Don't give in!"

"Oh, you fool, don't you know we're finally caught? We're caught. There'll be four armed securities in each one of those vehicles."

"What about Thomas? I thought he was going to do something. You said—"

"Not here." Connor's voice was grim. "It wasn't to have been here. We're just caught, Mike. That's it."

"We'll die fighting!" she insisted, her face a white oblong in the fuzzy black halo.

"The kids—" He jerked his head toward the rear of the van, from which soft weeping could be heard. "They'll be spared, anyway."

"For what? —No, don't you decelerate—" as the van began to slow to the speed of the plodding threat in front of them.

"I'm not," he told her wryly. "It's its little brain. Adjusting so as not to run over its brother—"

"I will not go down this way!" she screamed. "Do your thing— override it, do one of your broadcaster tricks—" and, with a lunge she yanked the steering hard to the right, as if to bypass the authority van. Ruth moaned in harmony with Catherine's wail of despair as the engine shut itself down.

Mike huddled into a small knot in her seat and stared at Connor, who shook his head with bemused frustration as the vans closed in. "Broadcaster trick to remember, Mike: You put your hands on top of the driver's, not on the steering."

ii

AUTHORITY ALWAYS wore white. Catherine, watching the approaching figures, recalled comments Victoria had made about that, about it being such a trite, old-fashioned statement, recalled David's defense of the agency, recalled the rationale of rebellious teenagers like Victoria wearing it: Prisoners, she'd said after bleaching her hair, just prisoners of authority, dressed in prison clothes. And, then, she thought they looked like biochem workers circling the van to clean up dangerous contaminations.

And we're the contaminants.

The third transport was approaching now in reverse as it neared the necklace of guards. They were all similar, Catherine noticed, all like the white-clad securities at the dome the day before—no, two days earlier, she realized; it had already been two days, spent huddling together, hiding, running.

They were all short-haired, even the women, all of a certain height, all smooth-faced, expressionless. All armed with large, shiny charge weapons which they held out in front of them with both hands and pointed at the van.

The third transport ground slowly to a halt, wheels gritting on the pavement. Through the back window they saw cold, set faces watching them before the rear doors were flung open and those faces too advanced. Except for Victoria's muffled gulps, there was utter silence inside; even the baby had stopped fretting and watched what was going on.

There were gestures, waving motions with the charge guns as if the securities were pushing cobwebs away. Their faces still emotionless, they gazed into the van. "Get out," one of them on the left said loudly but politely.

"Efficient to the end," Connor said. "All traffic stopped. Even the southbound lanes. They gridded us, blocked off the electromag up and down, like cutting out a bad—"

"Out," the security urged, still polite but now louder.

Mike whispered, "No."

"Yes. We played our hand as well as we could." Connor shrugged, unbuckled his restraint. "They won't destroy us, not if we surrender—they don't do that anymore—and Catherine will have to negotiate for those kids. Show some dignity, Mike. They never dealt with anybody like us. They're uncertain what we might do. Treat 'em like you did those fools on campus."

"Fools are human. I don't know how to deal with machines."

Another insistent gesticulation.

He turned around, a wry smile turning up the edges of his mouth. "I'm sorry, Catherine. Mother. Gather up what you can take for the baby."

"So it's really—" Catherine stopped.

He shrugged again. "We did pretty well."

Ruth sighed and turned to Victoria, telling her quietly to stuff certain things into the tote. "But the compcorder—" Victoria mumbled, and at Ruth's silent urging she shoved it into the very bottom and covered it with the makeshift diapers and snacks. Catherine clasped Virginia against her, observing for a moment the color of the baby's skin against her own. Connor lifted both hands, palms outward in a pleasantly cool gesture of surrender, and opened his door.

The securities moved in closer, two with Connor, another at the side of the van where Mike sat glaring at them through tangled black curls. Another pair motioned for Ruth to slide open her door; one gazed passively into the glass beside Victoria, who turned away under the inspection.

"Do you mind not scaring my children?"

The security pivoted around at Catherine's belligerent words. "You. Out."

"Get away from my daughter's face."

He laughed, gestured at her. Virginia still hugged against her, she leaned against Ruth's vehicle, scowling at the security. Another guard nudged Mike to stand beside her and next to Connor, whom one of the first pair was scanning with a metal detector now as the other stood guard, the charge gun held out like a divining rod. Catherine kept her eyes on the young man in front of her; he stared back insolently, eyes half-hidden by drooping eyelids.

"You're no better than university insurgents," she remarked. "They recruit you from there?"

"Be quiet."

Ruth and Victoria joined them, herded forward by the remaining two guards and subjected to the electronic sweep. Something alarmed: Victoria's bag.

The insolent one took it from her and rummaged deep. "It's

diapers. Food in metal cups," he scoffed.

Securities from the vehicle in front of them approached with wrist restraints; the driver, a heavyset, hairy man, swung himself out his door.

"Wait a minute." One of the guards hovering near Connor turned toward the driver. "Who're you?"

"Smithson. A-Six-One-Nine-Three. Deployed from ahead—" He ambled nearer, a charge gun in his right hand. The security glanced up the electromag, brought his suspicious gaze back to the heavy man and with one word— "Dissident!"—pressed a button that discharged a thick, white, hissing river of electricity that impaled the man upright, white puffs of smoke drifting out from several places in his body, smoke carrying the odor of cooked meat. In a millisecond the white river shut off, the other three securities who had climbed out the leading van were scrambling back inside, and Catherine huddled against the side of Ruth's vehicle, her arms around Virginia and Victoria as Mike and Ruth grasped each other, Connor shielding them.

"Rebels!" the insolent security screamed. Others from the remaining transports took assault positions near the front of the van.

"Get them inside!"

Catherine swore at the insolent guard—"Goddamn you!", an ancient oath her grandfather would say—as she and Victoria, Ruth and Connor and Mike were hauled into one of the two rear transports and ordered to sit in the back while their wrists were restrained. Catherine yelled: "I can't hold my child—" and, the female security coding the restraints fastened hers to a steel ring beside her, leaving her right hand free. Connor stared at the tubular electronic device that gleamed on his arms. A sudden tremendous blast of energy, a burst of sizzling light in front of them, and they watched the front van glitter with racing rivulets of electricity, heard shrieks from inside. The insolent guard sprinted back and threw himself into the driver's seat, shouting orders into the open communicator as a fourth fastened himself in on the other side.

"Cover! If there were four, there're probably forty. Net authority to trace how they got the transport. Override sensors. Speed one-thirty kilometers. Net authority to close down on-ramps. Buffalo facility prepared and apprised of situation."

The transport took off with a jerk, the polite electronic voice that advised caution abruptly silenced by the security in the passenger seat. The female guarding them raised wary eyes to the rear window occasionally where the second van followed close but otherwise regarded her prisoners contemptuously. Connor lifted his restrained arms to stretch.

"Down," the security ordered.

"I guess there was our last opportunity." Mike's voice was a whisper.

"I imagine."

"Quiet," the female guard said.

"Great vocabulary," Catherine told her.

The woman leaned into her face.

"The driver used lots of big words just now. You seem to know only one or two."

Victoria, trembling, said, "Mom..."

"Maybe they penalize you for using your brain? Or having one?" Catherine taunted. "Or maybe you're like any other common thug, and your wheels turn slow."

"Or maybe I don't have to say much, being the one with the weapon," the woman said, pushing Catherine's shoulder back against the seat. "Or maybe I wouldn't *have* anything to say to rabble like you." She gently pinched the flesh on Catherine's hand that supported Virginia's back. "You'll be lucky if they put out a release saying you were driven mad. That would be too kind, to shut you away for the rest of your life."

Catherine glared at her with calmness she didn't really feel. The other securities snickered. From the open communicator more chuckles from the second van behind them emanated eerily like ghostly electronic echoes.

"Or they might peddle tickets for a freak show, put you all in it, make lots and lots of money off you," the guard continued in an almost indistinguishable, eerie whisper. Connor's head snapped around, a sharp, penetrating scowl on his face. " 'The Golden Lunatics'—something like that. Haul you out on tour, cheap entertainment."

"Inappropriate communication. Tamp it down." That was from the transport behind them. A chuckle followed.

A soft gasp from the back of the transport where Victoria sat elicited a short, impatient cluck from the female security. "Grow up. You choose rebels for your company, this's what you get. One day all of you'll learn you're only destroying things. You'd bring down everything envireng's tried to build for half a century."

"You know what envireng did yesterday—day before—" Catherine stopped. "You don't care why we're here?"

"You're here—" the guard smirked and gestured circles— "because we got you!"

More chuckles echoed from the communicator. The insolent security wriggled cheerfully behind the steering and smiled.

iii

THIRTY-FIVE kilometers was nothing—such a small distance. Catherine considered that as she stared evenly at the female guard, who returned the gaze with a sardonic one of her own. Thirty-five kilometers, maybe fifteen minutes at the speed they were racing up the electromag. She looked for deliverance at each on-ramp as the moments counted down, thinking perhaps Thomas had arranged something there. They'd passed three, each blocked by several white transports, traffic backed up behind. After the third one she stopped expecting deliverance and clasped Virginia more tightly to her with her right arm, conscious that Mike was breathing hard, fast, next to her.

"Too quiet in here. Is it all right to have conversation? A little speculation?" Connor said.

"You don't have anything to speculate on. We have all the answers. Your speculation wouldn't line up with our answers."

"But let me ask anyway. What'll happen when we get to the Buffalo facility?"

"Whatever happens to people guilty of sedition, murder, fomenting rebellion."

"We're already guilty? And I thought there was still due process. How uninformed of me."

She smiled sardonically. "There are regulations."

"Ah, yes. Ethical."

"Beek," Virginia demanded, peering at the guard.

"She's thirsty," Victoria translated. "Can I reach in here and get—"

"No."

"You might express some sympathy for these children—this baby, she's not guilty of sedition or murder, and I'm sure you have compassion for a child exposed to the chemical, who's thirsty."

The woman's eyes flickered from Virginia back to Connor.

"Guess not," Connor remarked and turned toward his window.

"How much farther?" she asked the driver.

"Ten minutes to the facility."

She turned back to the prisoners, a satisfied look on her face. "Get her a drink. All your 'speculations,' Mr. Connor, will be irrelevant in ten minutes."

The automatic road signs had become functional in the late evening dim and, as the van crossed the sensors, blinked on to inform them that they'd arrived at Buffalo. Here in the Northeast there were no limb-strewn sidewalks or broken windows, no closed streets or eerily vacant houses. By now they would know about what had happened in the South, and yet, not being personally affected by it, they'd feel safe. A friendly, oblivious bustle manifested itself in the vans and transports hurrying through the streets, the exodus of workers returning to their stackhouses and apartments. Catherine wanted to shriek, to wave her right arm to draw the attention of some of the unaware citizens, but kept cold eyes on the guard. The vans wailed at crossing lights to alert other vehicles that they were in that moment proprietors of the avenues, and sped onward toward the border. Catherine sensed a change in Mike's respiration, a tightening in her body. She had turned from the window and with an unexpected leap was upon the guard, using her restrained arms and wrists like a single club. Connor yelled her name and threw himself off the seat, only to be flung back by the other guard, who held him still with the charge gun pressed into the middle of his breastbone. In a brief moment, the female guard had both hands on Mike's collar, Ruth's old robe bunched up under her chin.

"You may as well kill me—throw me out there, let something run over me—"

"You—" the woman slung her down beside Catherine— "you're not going anywhere. Be quiet. Sit still."

The tourist mecca that was the Falls was somewhere off to the left and a bit farther north, Catherine knew; Connor had intended to drive there, seem as other tourists and slip over into Canada unheeded. But now the securities turned abruptly west into the horizon of dying red light. Her weapon still trained on Mike, the female and the other guard conferred in a whispered word or two and left the rear of the transport to huddle over the shoulders of the pair in the front. Connor frowned, nudging his mother, and nodded slightly. Looming ahead was the stark white marble building of the sort envireng favored, a utilitarian, solid block symbolizing function, endurance, responsibility. Sitting like a disapproving, strict master at the exit, it seemed to watch the transports and vans as they edged past into Canada. Catherine glanced behind to see the set faces in the front of the covering van; both vehicles had slowed their pace at last as they approached the building. She sighed deeply and shut her eyes, but only a moment before the gathering outside of a number of authority officials, the brief, bracing rush of cool outside air into her face, and the explosion. The captives were held fast for a moment against their seats, and the van hurtled forward, past a fire that seemed to boil and bubble as the chemicals had, sliding down the glastique dome, consuming many of the envirengs and authorities. Connor jerked sideways to apprise what was happening behind them. The van which had followed them for thirty-five kilometers had slewed to a halt near the blazing bonfire that oozed along the pavement like lava. The driver of that van engaged the reverse gear and sped backwards. Turning to the front again, Connor and Catherine watched the insolent driver flick his finger against his thumb in obscene salute to a border official as he sped through the checkpoint without slowing down.

iv

VICTORIA'S YELPS filled the van for some time. "Oh! Oh!"

"That's as annoying as your bawling," the woman in white remarked.

The transport hurtled onward, speeding unimpeded through Fort Erie and northwest toward Hamilton and ultimately Toronto, where, their erstwhile guards told them, there were contacts informed at a broadcast station, ready to air interviews with William Connor of the United States. The driver and three insurgents who had commandeered the white van en route from Jamestown to intercept them south of Buffalo were uninterested in explaining to Mike how they'd managed to lure a trained security force of four into a trap and disarm them, and nor did they talk about where the legitimate four guards might be. After a prolonged stare from Connor, Mike leaned back against her seat and refrained from other questions.

Victoria babbled for a while longer, requesting their names, praising their cool, until another hard gaze from the journalist wrung silence from her as well. When the van became peaceful and reflective, the woman softly detailed conditions under which they'd have their freedom: "You know Canada's never reinstated the extradition treaty with the United States. Once you leave this vehicle, you're liberated. You will not disclose to anybody, ever, any description of us. You will not betray the route you took, or the help along the way."

The precisely chosen words brought solemnity to Victoria's and even Mike's faces. The woman regarded them with assessing eyes. "Some of you'll be tempted to, you'll want to brag about having outwitted the great authority. If you're one of those, do the others a favor and go off on your own. Remember: You simply got over the border. They'll know about that, sure, but they won't be able to put other pieces together unless you tell them. You cannot do it. Treaty or no treaty, there are silent-report envirengs scattered in Canada. They have ways of bringing talkative insurgents back over the border. So starting now, you have two choices: Either become completely anonymous, never explain anything to anyone; or make use of the contacts and occupation of Mr. Connor and publish your story prominently and become immune that way. There's nothing in between. Casual, offhand discussion of what happened to you, bragging about it, relying on loyalties which, I assure you, may be false as many times as they're not, will result in your return home. In a transport with real guards." She paused. "Anything you want to know that we *can* tell you?"

"Where will you take us?" Connor said.

"Straight to that broadcast station. They'll upload that compcorder of yours," she said to Victoria, "the one we know you have. Then we all leave—" she unfastened several of the tight-fix fasteners on the front of the white uniform to uncover a hint of plaid fabric— "and turn into Canadian citizens. We walk away from each other. No backward looks."

"You go home?" Victoria ventured.

The woman smiled enigmatically and turned away.

The driver skirted Hamilton and skimmed Lake Ontario, steering northeast now in the darkness of the Canadian highway. Catherine was weary from trying to push away the questions that sprang to her mind: Where would she be able to reach her parents?

How would she transport the two girls across the vast provinces if she had to? And then, how would she learn—how would she know—what had happened inside her and Virginia? She closed her eyes to shut out the dim light that animated the thoughts. The baby awoke and clamored for something to drink, which Connor gave her this time.

Toronto gleamed from afar, a bristly, acicular gem sitting upon a lacy fiber of glittering lights tracing patterns at the edge of the water. The people in the transport sat in reflective silence as they crossed into the city and, slowing to the limits that flashed sternly at them as they approached too fast, edged through avenues moving with slower traffic now that work hours were done. Catherine turned to ask Connor or Mike what their intentions were but found them staring outward. Ruth played her finger games with the baby, and Victoria, in spite of herself, was napping. Catherine wanted especially to awaken Victoria, to ask her the question most bothersome, the one that popped up over and over and couldn't be suppressed. The one about David. She reached for the school-issue tote more than once and, at last drawing Connor's attention and sudden raised eyebrows, settled back to return his stare, the tote unopened.

A few final turns brought them to the service entrance of the broadcast station, its bright lights forbidding shadows and secrecy in its vicinity. The transport slowed to a crawl.

"Be careful stepping out," the woman said softly, swinging her door open.

"Thank you." Catherine, the baby clinging to her, clambered outside, followed by the suddenly alert Victoria who slung the tote onto her back. Connor was last, shoving Mike ahead of him.

"No dawdling." He urged them inside the portal. Catherine turned to peer at the transport, which had come to a halt in the darker edges of the street up ahead. Connor prodded her through the doorway.

"I had no idea they..."

"What they said about peddling tickets, making money off us, you think securities would ever say anything like that? And then they never even looked into Victoria's bag. Even when it set off the alarm."

Four conservatively-clad young people emerged from the transport up ahead. Immediately separating into pairs, they walked into warmly glowing shops down the avenue. The white van was ghostly and desolate.

v

THE STATION managers had not after all been prepared sufficiently. The six Americans found themselves surrounded by a growing crowd of interns and journalists who at first seemed not to know what questions to ask, how to handle them, whether to demand details about their escape, which, as the insurgents had said, had already been reported publicly. Mike thrust out her chin and argued, the incongruous robe flapping and displaying more of her body than Catherine would have found comfortable, if she'd been wearing it. Connor blinked in the harsh lighting, lines creasing his unprepped face. In the midst of the chaos, Victoria said, "*Diabhalta!*" and ripped open the tote, the sound another attention-grabbing slash that cut off the voices. In the silence she unlocked and opened one file, handed Connor the compcorder as if it were an expensive gift.

He turned to the other reporters. "This is what you need."

"Only that one file. I didn't uncode anything else," Victoria said. "Get it, and then I want it back."

Someone gestured for everyone to go down a hallway to a small office from which the crowd spilled outward as Connor uploaded Victoria's file, with her supervising, into the station's information system. Catherine, Mike, and Ruth stood aside until Connor gestured for Mike to join him.

"This is Micaela Sánchez; she can augment the file with additional details..." Whatever else he intended to say was drowned out as the crowd repeated her name and asked questions. Victoria slid the compcorder quickly away. Ruth and Catherine recoiled when gazes fell upon them as Connor explained their part of the journey.

The technical crew discussed the disadvantages of cleaning Connor and Mike up before interviewing them. "Makeup, but not too much," Connor suggested. "We just got away from terrorists and a storm and being deranged." He smiled, paused to acknowledge the laughs.

Catherine and Ruth began edging away, shielding Victoria and the baby. Connor noticed, jogged over, took Ruth's arm. "Where are you two going? They may want to talk with you."

"Oh, no. No. This is your part. Go do your job."

"But, wait...you shouldn't leave yet. How'll you get anywhere without transport? You'll be easy to spot, wandering around, asking for help."

Victoria interrupted irritably, "We're in Canada. We don't have to ask for help now. Anyway, we have cellcomm back again."

One of the journalists reading Victoria's file heard the questions and pulled himself away from his screen, offered the use of his own vehicle. It was leased anyway, he said offhandedly. They could return it at one of the rental facilities scattered throughout the province.

Catherine started saying, "What about Manitoba?" but stopped at Connor's loud interruption and hearty gratitude: "Generous of you."

The manager had also been listening. "It would be great to have an interview with the young lady there."

From behind Ruth, Victoria said, "No." Just the one syllable; but the man raised his brows and asked nothing else. Catherine considered yelling one of her grandfather's swear words again; it might mean more to them, here, might not be received with mocking sneers as just the juvenile expression of an uneducated person—the way they'd react back home, she knew: Such a petty, puerile waste of speech.

She wondered how much these journalists had really absorbed yet of the file; did they understand in even a simple way why she had to travel onward, while she could? She knew there wasn't any point trying to explain today. Eventually Connor would get past his primary goal of delivering a powerful presentation; it was the foremost thing animating him right now, his focus. He'd reverted to Newsman. She could tell. And Mike would start to think beyond vengeance, beyond explaining chemicals and history and what fools they were in that overarching agency, Environmental Engineering, whose very name showed its plodding determination to arrange every single stage of their lives.

On envireng's terms.

But right now she and Ruth knew what had to be done next.

"It's time to leave," she said. Ruth nodded once, gently nudged Victoria towards the exit.

Connor spoke to the journalists: "Give me a minute—" and, one arm around Ruth's waist and the other on Catherine's shoulder, where Virginia picked at his fingers, he led them a few paces away from the room from which inquisitive eyes stared.

"What are you doing?"

"If I stay too long here, it might get hard, going on, getting away. I wish I could care more, like you and Mike. I just want to get the girls somewhere safe. I'm just tired. You do what you have to."

"That's what made everything the way it is." Mike paced a few steps back and forth in the broad hallway, spoke fiercely. The journalists behind her stared. " 'You do it, I don't want to, it's hard.' That's all you've said, once you got her back." She gestured at Victoria.

"Shut up, Mike."

"Don't tell me—"

But it was Catherine who broke in this time: "Don't tell her to shut up. She's not wrong. But I'm not the one to do what she wants done. Yes, *you* do it," she told Mike. "Try as hard as you want. You'll see."

"Oh, it'll change. Sometime. People know what's wrong. *You* know." Connor shrugged. "I know."

She laughed a short, scornful laugh, remembering Ruth's apartment. "Good luck to you both."

"No such thing as luck."

"Oh, no," she said grimly. "No luck. Not even bad luck."

"I'll arrange..." He touched his temple with a finger.

"And you'll do it yourself, not trust someone else to?"

"You know I will. How about—" he paused, closed his eyes as if to focus on a map she couldn't see. "Kenora? Will that work?"

"Kenora."

"Remember me to your parents."

She started to object—he'd never known her parents, how could she remember him to them? His steady gaze at her brought another thought to her mind...the tune she'd hummed and sung.

"Impossible," she told him.

He turned to Ruth. "So how'll I find you, Mother?"

"Or maybe how'll I find *you*. But you'll be *here*. I'll bring the car back for that kind man."

"That kind man probably recoded it off another journalist somewhere. A broadcaster's—"

"—broadcaster's trick." Mike had wandered closer to them.

"We know."

"Are you going to stick around, keep him honest?" Ruth asked.

"For a while. And then I'll be doing my thing. We don't get along, I'm sure you noticed. After we air it, he can find you, and I'll—I don't know...." She gazed at the blank wall, her face troubled and very young, and turned abruptly back to the larger room, a flip of her hand indicating her farewell.

The manager approached: "We're going to interrupt programming with a special announcement—you'll need to come with us, Mr. Connor."

"Fine, all right—" Connor brushed off the solicitous hand with irritation. Rummaging in a pocket of the dark exercise shirt Mike had found for him long ago, it seemed long ago, at the university, he drew out something and pressed it into Catherine's free hand, closing her fingers over it. "He wanted it returned to you."

The coins were warm and moist in her palm.

He shifted his shoulders around as if they ached. "Mother, take care of yourself and her and those children." He hugged her, pulled back, seemed to want to say more and stopped, looking into her face with what Catherine thought resembled guilt. Or shame.

"Catherine—you're certain about that address?"

"I always know where they are."

"Be careful. —All right!" he yelled at the manager who'd gestured again. A long pause, and then Catherine turned her back to him and walked away, Ruth and Victoria at her side.

Subtropical Depression

THE AIR was much cooler in northern Ontario. They lowered the car's windows and let the brisk, chill breeze flood the vehicle with blasts of oxygen, for the sheer pleasure of it—so they told each other, but Victoria shivered. Ruth drove, and as they traversed the province, along the fringy edges of Georgian Bay to Sudbury, then flying along the North Channel to Sault Ste. Marie, ever north, ever west, Catherine played with Virginia as if they were on the long-planned vacation to the beach and it were David driving, steering them past sights they could store in those deep places in their minds and retrieve later in the dreary hours of frugal, responsible economy. Victoria ran her hands through the emu-feather hair, pulling ends forward to look skeptically at them. Perhaps Mike's fashion judgment was giving her second thoughts.

They did not stop except for refueling, and to go to the bathroom, a need Victoria felt more keenly than the others. Catherine still imagined envireng following their movements. But the juices and drinks, crackers and wafers they had packed in Columbia and at Thomas's fueling station were gone, left behind in Ruth's van somewhere south of Buffalo, except for the few Victoria had crammed into the tote. At last, reluctantly, they used the posted account number of whatever journalist it was who'd leased the vehicle, and replenished their supplies at a food stop.

By early morning Connor's interviews, substantiated with the information Victoria had stolen, were airing on every station they scanned. Ruth approved of the tone of his indignant voice filling the car with details of the envireng agency. Then they laughed when Mike's profanities were broadcast, after Connor's somber delivery. In mid-morning there came an alert—an emergency assembly of directors of several of the agencies who answered to the Executive Council.

They listened and drove on. Shortly after lunch, unless Connor had been unsuccessful, they would meet Catherine's mother and father in Kenora. Catherine mutely urged Ruth to hurry, and rubbed her arms more often now as odd prickling tingles crossed over them. Virginia climbed upon her lap, laid her head down and slept fitfully in the sunlight glaring through the windows. Once in a while she whimpered as from a bad dream.

They raised the side glasses. The air had become a bit crisp, and Victoria claimed to be positively freezing. Mindful of the baby's nap, weary of talking, more aware now of losses, she tapped at her compcorder, drew up eerie, wailing music, the sort her age group liked these days. Catherine gazed at Ruth's thick gray hair, now disarrayed, her posture confident and energetic, her arms and hands golden in the sunlight. Her shoulders quivering sometimes with passing tremors.

The music was too haunting. "Please stop," she told Victoria brusquely. "Do something else. No. Pull up the files. I want you to tell me something."

Victoria eyed her warily and cut off the quavering notes. "What do you want to know?"

"Who sold off the stockpiled Eutopix?"

"I don't know." The voice was sullen—the old Victoria again, shoulders hunched protectively.

"Your father. David wanted us to enjoy our holiday. He didn't, wouldn't have—"

"What?" The syllable was challenging, irritated.

"Just to give us something nice?"

Victoria turned her back impassively and resumed playing the haunting music as the car sped onward to Kenora.